Mia was overwhelmed by all the emotions she was experiencing. Desire was one thing that she could handle. This was something else—a feeling of security, trust…family.

Mia felt Keylan's hand rise from her shoulder and land in her hair, where he removed the clip and placed it on the small table that sat behind the sofa, allowing Mia's hair to fall free.

"What are you doing?" she whispered, trying not to disturb Colby, who had his eyes closed.

"I prefer it this way. Do you have a problem with that?" he asked, running his fingers through her curls.

"No," she uttered, looking up into his passion-filled eyes. She raised her chin, offering herself to him, and Keylan didn't hesitate.

Keylan leaned down and kissed her gently on the lips. He cupped Mia's face with his right hand and the kiss became more passionate. Colby stirred and Keylan dropped his hand and leaned his forehead against hers. Mia whispered, "I thought I was in this alone."

"Not hardly…"

Dear Reader,

I hope you enjoyed the first installment in The Kingsleys of Texas series, *Always My Baby*. It is with great pleasure that I introduce you to the youngest member of the family, Keylan "KJ" Kingsley. Not all the Kingsley heirs accept the destiny set forward by their birth.

They say love and basketball don't mix. In *An Unexpected Holiday Gift*, Keylan Kingsley and Mia Ramirez seem to agree. However, their undeniable attraction to each other and the developing bond between Keylan and Mia's young son tells a very different story.

I love interacting with my readers, so please let me know how you liked Keylan and Mia's story and look out for what's in store for the only married Kingsley son. Let's see if love and marriage can survive secrets and blackmail. You can follow and contact me on Facebook or Twitter, @KennersonBooks.

Peace and love,

Martha

AN UNEXPECTED
Holiday Gift

MARTHA KENNERSON

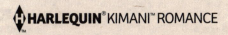
HARLEQUIN® KIMANI™ ROMANCE

Recycling programs
for this product may
not exist in your area.

ISBN-13: 978-0-373-86527-7

An Unexpected Holiday Gift

Copyright © 2017 by Martha Kennerson

For questions and comments about the quality of this book please contact us
at CustomerService@Harlequin.com.

Printed in U.S.A.

Martha Kennerson's love of reading and writing is a significant part of who she is, and she uses both to create the kinds of stories that touch your heart. Martha lives with her family in League City, Texas, and believes her current blessings are only matched by the struggle it took to achieve such happiness. To find out more about Martha and her journey, check out her website at marthakennerson.com.

Books by Martha Kennerson

Harlequin Kimani Romance

Protecting the Heiress
Seducing the Heiress
Tempting the Heiress
Always My Baby
An Unexpected Holiday Gift

I'd like to dedicate this book to my eight-year-old muse, Keylan. Thank you for not only letting me "borrow" your name for my hero, but also allowing me to share with the world parts of your personal journey.
It's such an honor to be able to show just how cool and special a kid with Down syndrome can be.

Chapter 1

Keylan Kingsley walked in a circle, admiring his surroundings before coming to a stand in the middle of the large NBA-inspired gym outfitted with an oversize scoreboard and arena-style seating. Standing with his legs slightly apart, bouncing a basketball, he wore a black handmade Italian suit, a taupe-colored collarless shirt, black loafers and dark aviator sunglasses.

He looked up and scanned the ceiling, admiring all the banners that hung overhead; thirty of them, to be exact. They all represented championships won by various community leagues that this foundation supported. Keylan's mind flashed back to a time when he'd played on one of those community championship teams and the memory made him smile.

"My, how time flies," Keylan murmured to himself, placing the ball on the floor.

"Yes, it does. May I help you with something, Mr. Kingsley?" a sweet voice asked.

Keylan James Kingsley, or KJ, as he was known by his family, friends and legions of fans, was the youngest son and only heir to the Kingsley family's billion-dollar oil and gas conglomerate who chose not to follow his siblings into the business. The twenty-six-year-old basketball star was a marquee player for the Houston Carriers.

Keylan turned toward the sound and his breath caught in his throat. He felt like he'd just been hit in the chest by a wayward basketball. *Damn! She's stunning...and fine, too. This might not be so bad, after all.* "I certainly hope so, little momma," he proclaimed, offering up a sexy smile, removing his sunglasses and placing them in the inside pocket of his jacket.

The beautiful woman standing several feet away wore blue jeans and a white T-shirt, both splattered with green and yellow paint. She rolled her eyes skyward, dropped her shoulders and placed her left hand on her hip. "I may be petite, Mr. Kingsley, but I'm certainly not your mother," she replied. Her voice had a sharp edge to its tone.

Maybe I spoke too soon. "My apologies." Keylan raised both hands in surrender. "You have me at a disadvantage. You know me but I don't think I've had the pleasure, although you do look familiar."

"Mia Ramirez," said the feisty, olive-skinned beauty.

"I'm pleased to make your acquaintance. You missed a spot," he said, pointing at the pristine-white tennis shoes she wore.

Mia looked down briefly before returning her gaze to Keylan, where she gifted him with a wide smile that lit up her eyes. It was as if she'd just experienced a pleasant memory.

Wow! "So...is it Ms. or Mrs. Ramirez?" he asked with a slightly raised left eyebrow.

"I'm the foundation's activities director. What can I do for you, Mr. Kingsley?" she replied, dropping her smile, clearly unwilling to answer his not so subtle question.

Keylan set his mouth in a tight line. His legendary charm clearly wasn't having an effect on Mia Ramirez. By now he should have her number, address and be making plans to meet up later. He gave his head a slow shake, pushed out a quick breath and said, "I have some mandatory community service hours I need to—"

"Let me guess," Mia interrupted, nodding as she slowly walked toward him. "You'd like me to work with your assistant or someone to set up some type of photo opportunity with the kids where you come in and present us with a check." She stopped and stood two feet in front of Keylan.

"Well—"

"No, wait. I got it." Mia held up her left index finger and her nose crinkled as though she'd just encountered a foul smell. "You have a couple of signed balls you want to give me to auction off for the proceeds. You get a photo op, the hours you need, of course, and I get a big check…literally."

Mia might look like a kid with the cute high ponytail and minimal makeup she wore, but looks were deceiving. Keylan folded his arms across his chest and stared down at Mia. "Seems like you already have a set of brass ones. You certainly don't need any additional balls from me."

Mia's mouth flew open but quickly closed as she matched his stance. They stood glaring at each other in silence. While Keylan liked Mia's moxie, he didn't know what angered him more: the fact that she'd made such judgmental assumptions about him or, given his time restraints lately and the fact that he hadn't spent much time in a place he loved so much, that she had every right to question his sincerity. Keylan's aunt Elizabeth ran their foundation and had been trying to get him to spend more time there for years.

Keylan dropped his arms. "Look, Ms….Mrs.… whatever—"

"Mia is fine," she offered.

"I'm not here to put on some show and get out of doing

my community service. In fact, until about—" he checked the time on his Bulgari Diagono watch "—eight minutes ago, I was really looking forward to spending time here… with the kids."

Mia dropped her arms and shifted her weight from one foot to the other. "Well, if you're serious about putting in some real time here, we could always use a few extra reliable hands. I think our kids would love seeing you, too."

"But clearly not you." Keylan smirked.

"My personal feelings aren't important. This is your family's foundation…you can come and go as you please. Besides, you really don't want to know what I think," she murmured, turning to walk away.

"Oh, but I do," he assured her.

Mia turned back to face Keylan and placed her fingertips in her pants' pockets. "I wouldn't want to insult my boss's nephew right to his face." She smirked.

"It's a bit late for that, don't you think? I'm a big boy—I can handle it." Keylan leaned forward. "And I can keep a secret." Keylan returned to his full height.

Mia smiled. "In my experience, Mr. Kingsley, men like you—"

Keylan tilted his head slightly to the right. "Men like me?" He ignored his buzzing cell phone.

"Yes, men too busy for their own good. Do you need to get that?" she said, gesturing toward his pocket with her head.

"No, please continue," he insisted.

"Men that think the world revolves around them. Men that think they can simply smile, lie, buy or flirt their way out of doing the right thing. Men like that—" Mia mirrored his tilted head "—don't care about anything or anyone but themselves, and they certainly don't have time for a bunch of kids they don't know whose families can't afford to buy their child's favorite sports player's overpriced shoes that they had made overseas for three dollars."

"Wow." Keylan circled Mia, coming to stand behind her. He leaned forward, ignoring the sweet scent of vanilla radiating from her petite body and the rise and fall of her breasts making his crotch suddenly uncomfortable, and spoke softly. "Good thing I'm not one of those men."

"We'll see," she said, taking a step forward and turning to face him. Keylan's phone buzzed again. "You sure you don't need to get that?"

Probably. However, I won't give you the satisfaction. "No, I'm good. When and where do we start?"

"If you follow me to the office, we can go over the schedule."

"After you."

Mia turned and Keylan couldn't help but admire her firm backside as his body reacted instantly. *Calm down, boy...not just yet.*

"Did you say something?" Mia asked and stopped, looking over her shoulders.

Did I say that out loud? "No, but what's with the paint?"

Mia smirked. "We were painting one of the smaller rooms. It got...messy."

"I guess you weren't wearing those tennis shoes."

"Nope, socks." Mia started back toward her office.

"Wait. Why were you painting a room? I can't believe my aunt wouldn't hire someone to handle that for you."

Mia laughed and the sound sent a strange feeling throughout his body. "It was more of a fun activity for the kids than a real painting job, but you're right, your aunt wouldn't have allowed such a thing to happen."

"Now, that I can believe." Keylan scanned the halls as they proceeded. "Some things never change."

"Pardon me?"

"Thanksgiving was last week and this place is already decked out like Santa's workshop, with Christmas still several weeks away. The Christmas tree at the front entrance is beautiful, by the way. I love all the kids' ornaments on it."

"Yes, the decorators were here first thing Friday morning." Mia visibly forced a smile. "I'm just glad they used the stuff the kids made. They would have been very disappointed."

Mia could feel Keylan's eyes on her as they made their way down the quite long hall. She couldn't understand how such an arrogant man, king of the playboys and known as an aggressive player on the basketball court, could have her body responding in a way it hadn't in years. So what if he was tall, with a sun-kissed tan, and handsome beyond reason? Why had her breath caught in her throat at the sight of him, and why had the sudden ache and weight of her breasts made Mia think she was wearing the wrong size bra?

It had been years since twenty-six-year-old Mia had been even remotely attracted to anyone. It wasn't as if she didn't like men; it was just that dating and sex wasn't a priority of the mother to a four-year-old boy with Down syndrome. Mia hated the idea that it was Keylan that had awakened her dormant and sexually deprived body. To make things worse, she'd basically insulted her boss's nephew to his face. *Nice going, Mia.*

Mia led Keylan into a midsize office several doors down from the gym. An oak desk with a salt finish sat on the right side of the room across from a large bay window that looked out over the playground. A dry-erase calendar on the wall behind Mia's desk outlined the year-long activities that were in several different stages of planning.

"Please have a seat, Mr. Kingsley," she said, taking a seat behind her desk.

The left wall of custom shelves was filled with a few personal photos and years of memorabilia from the many events and activities she'd conducted, along with awards she'd received during her tenure. "It's Keylan, or KJ, if you prefer," he said, admiring all the objects on her shelves. "How long have you worked for my family?"

"Almost five years," she replied to his back, trying to ignore the way his perfectly cut suit draped his Greek-god-like physical form.

"I can't believe we haven't met before, especially since you're the one who organized the annual three-on-three basketball tournaments, the charity bowling and the Holiday Toys for Tots drive. Those are our three biggest charity events."

"I started right after you were drafted into the NBA. How do you know that I was the one who organized those events?" she asked, her forehead creased.

Keylan turned toward her, pointing at the awards she'd received from both the mayor of Houston and several city council members. "It says so right here."

"Oh…yeah, well, I'm usually working the events, which means I'm too busy to enjoy them." Mia shook her mouse to wake up her computer so she could check her emails. "If you can direct your attention to the whiteboard, we can see what we can do to get you the hours you need."

Keylan folded his six-foot-five-inch frame and took a seat in one of the oval, white leather chairs in front of her desk. "Why weren't you at last year's toy drive event?"

"How do you know I wasn't?"

"Because I was there and I would have remembered you." He smiled, showing off a perfect set of white teeth. "Plus, my mother and aunt personally thanked everyone there for all their hard work. So…why weren't you there?"

"I only have to organize the toy drive. I'm not required

to work it. Plus, I had other plans. Besides, I'm not a big fan of all the pomp and circumstance the holiday brings."

Keylan sat forward. "*What*? You don't like all the decorations, the lights, the parties, all those presents? Or is it a religious thing for you?"

"I take it you do."

"Of course."

"No, it's not a religious thing," she replied, shaking her head. "I think celebrating Christmas is fine—it's just not my favorite time of year," she explained.

"There's got to be a story there," he concluded.

"There isn't, and my assistant, Sandra, prefers to work that particular event."

"You call me, boss lady?" Sandra asked as she entered the room wearing blue jeans and a white T-shirt with the words Kingsley Foundation printed in large red letters across it. She came to a quick stop after catching sight of Keylan.

"No. But since you're here…Sandra White, this is—"

"KJ. I know who he is," she replied, flipping her sandy-blond hair off her shoulder. Sandra looked at Mia as though she had insulted her intelligence.

"Pleased to meet you," Keylan said, standing and offering his hand.

"Nice to meet you, too." Sandra accepted his hand, giving it a slow shake while smiling and batting her green eyes.

Mia's phone rang as she stood, watching Sandra's embarrassing display of amorous behavior.

"No worries, I'll get the phone." Mia rolled her eyes as she picked up the receiver. "Mia Ramirez."

Sandra slowly withdrew her hand and smiled. "Can I get you anything, KJ? Coffee, tea, soda, my number?"

Keylan smiled. "Thanks, I'm fine."

"Yes, you are," Sandra offered, her smile widening.

"Sandra, Dr. Bissell's assistant is on line one. Can you please take down the names of his guests for this weekend's charity bowling tournament?"

"Sure. Nice meeting you, KJ," she said, backing out of the office.

"Where were we?" Mia asked, not really expecting an answer.

"You were about to tell me why you don't like Christmas."

Mia frowned. "I never said I didn't like Christmas, and we were about to review the schedule to see how we can accommodate your needs."

A slow, sexy smile crawled across Keylan's face and Mia quickly regretted the last words in her statement.

"I have a few ideas."

"I bet you do," she murmured.

Keylan pointed to the whiteboard. "I was referring to those two events."

Mia prayed her face wasn't as red as her nail polish. "Yes, of course. How many hours do you need?"

"Eighty."

Mia reached for the tablet that sat on the edge of her desk but Keylan beat her to it. When his hand touched hers, their eyes collided and a shock of desire hit Mia like a runaway train. She slowly withdrew her hand and accepted the tablet. "Th-thank you."

"You're welcome."

Mia cleared her throat. "So, you want to work the toy drive and the charity bowling tournament. If you work the whole time, for both of these events, you will earn sixteen hours." She ran her fingers across the keys, making note of his request. "That leaves sixty-four hours that you'll still need to earn."

"I realize that, which is why I'd like to earn the rest of those hours working here."

"Here." Mia waved her hand in the air.

"Yes, here. It is my family's foundation, remember. I'm thinking—" Keylan rubbed his hands together "—twenty hours a week."

"Twenty…a week…here? Doing what exactly?" *Other than making me crazy.*

Keylan turned in his chair and looked at the whiteboard. "I was thinking I'd help out with the kids' round-up." He turned back to Mia and smiled.

"The kids' round-up? Do you have any idea what that is…what's required?"

Keylan sighed. "Believe it or not, I used to spend a lot of time here. Unless things have changed, this is helping with just about every activity you can think of with the kids. Helping with homework, story time for the little ones, sports—you name it."

"No, nothing's changed, that's it. And how do you plan to make such a commitment with your busy professional and personal schedule?" *No, you didn't just say that out loud, Mia.*

Keylan's left eyebrow quirked and he smirked. "Why don't you let me worry about my schedule?"

"Fine. When would you like to get started?"

"Well, according to the schedule, you have a group of kids about to have a basketball game in twenty minutes."

"Those are the kids in our after-school Latch Key program. Coach Wanda and her kids would love having a NBA star in their midst."

"Great." Keylan raised his right hand and used his thumb to point behind him. "I'll just go get changed."

Mia checked her watch. "Will you be able to get back in time? It's important to stay on schedule with these kids."

Keylan frowned. "Where am I going?"

"You'll want to go change."

"The last time I checked, the locker rooms were on the other side of the gym," he said, smiling. "I keep a change of clothes in my car."

Mia smirked. "I bet you do."

Keylan scratched his chin with his left thumb. "You're determined to think the worst of me, aren't you?" He shook his head. "Between my rehab and ever-changing practice schedule, I have to stay prepared."

"Oh…" *Nice going, Mia.*

Keylan stood. "Should I go change?"

"Please." Mia rose from her chair. "I know Coach Wanda will appreciate the help and I'm sure you'll do a great job."

"I'm not sure you really believe that but I guess we'll see," he said, heading out of the office.

Yes, we will.

Chapter 2

Keylan quickly changed into a pair of black-and-blue knee-length shorts, a blue T-shirt and his own branded black-and-blue sneakers. He passed a much smaller gym that had been retrofitted to accommodate young children with disabilities. The walls were padded from the floor halfway up the wall and half the floors were padded, as well. The basketball hoop had been lowered to five feet and the court was halved. Keylan remembered how proud he'd felt when his aunt decided to use all the recommendations he'd made for the specialized gym. He'd always known how important it was for all kids to have a safe place to play. The pictures he'd seen didn't do the final project justice.

The sound of children's laughter and a whistle being blown captured his attention. Keylan stood at the wood Dutch door, its top half open, and watched ten young children playing. Their laughter and exaggerated expressions of excitement stopped him short.

"May I help you, sir?" questioned a pretty young blonde holding a bright yellow ball.

"Hi, I'm Keylan Kingsley—"

"KJ, what are you doing over here?" Sandra asked. "I thought you were working with Coach Wanda."

"I was until I ran across these cool kids," he replied to

an approaching Sandra before turning back to the laughing children. One little boy with a head full of curly brown hair caught his attention. He was trying to maneuver a ball twice his size and Keylan was impressed by his determination.

"Yes, they are. This is the Down's class from our special needs school," Sandra explained.

"I didn't realize the Down's class had gotten so big. I knew our foundation school was growing, but I had no idea just how much."

"Yep, and that's due in large part to the efforts of this wonderful lady," she proudly proclaimed. "Coach Cathy Hooper, this is KJ. He plays for the Houston Carriers."

"Yes, I know. Nice to meet you," Coach Hooper said, her face flushed.

"The pleasure is mine," he replied.

"KJ will be helping out here from time to time." Sandra turned back to KJ. "Follow me. I'll take you to Coach Wanda. She's in the big gym."

"Actually, I think I'd like to spend some time with these guys right now. Can you see if it'll be okay for me to come by later this afternoon?"

"Sure."

He turned to Coach Hooper and gifted her with a megawatt smile. "That is, if you don't mind a little help?"

"Of course not. But are you sure you want to work with my kids?" She looked over her shoulder and laughed as several of the kids chased her assistant. Coach Hooper returned her attention to Keylan. "They're beautiful, sweet and a whole lot of fun, but I'm not sure they'll be interested in basketball."

"They don't have to be," Keylan assured her. He reached across the door, unlocked it and let himself in. "We can do whatever they want, but I might surprise you with what I have in mind."

"Well, welcome…"

"I guess I'll go talk to Coach Wanda," Sandra informed him as she turned to leave.

Keylan stood back and watched as six little boys, no more than six or seven years old, played their version of dodgeball. Three girls, roughly the same age as the boys, chased each other on large bouncy balls with handles. They all wore white foundation T-shirts, khaki shorts and tennis shoes, and laughed and played together as if they didn't have a care in the world.

In the corner of the room Keylan spotted the small, curly-haired boy he'd noticed earlier. He couldn't have been more than five years old. The boy stood with a ball nearly as big as he was, bouncing it against the wall. It was a game of catch that Keylan remembered playing often himself; only he'd used two basketballs.

Keylan tilted his head and smiled whenever the little boy lost control of the ball and would fall backward on the matted floor. The look of determination on the boy's face made Keylan's heart expand and he was filled with a sense of pride for the child whenever he caught the ball and stayed upright.

He walked over to the area where they played, knelt down on one knee and introduced himself to all of the children. The boys that had been tossing the ball back and forth were excited to meet him, as were the three girls. Keylan figured it was more curiosity about his height rather than the acknowledgment of him being a professional basketball player. However, the small boy wouldn't come anywhere near Keylan. When all the children returned to their games under the watchful eye of Coach Hooper and her assistant, Keylan tried to talk to the little boy. To no avail.

He decided to take another approach. Keylan selected a basketball from the wire basket, laid his back flat on the floor and began tossing the ball he'd selected into the air with both hands. Before long he was joined on the mat by several of the children. Soon, all but the shy boy were on the mat, tossing their balls into the air. He stood back, holding his ball tightly to his chest and watching as Keylan tossed his from one hand to the other.

"Hi, my name is Keylan," he introduced himself, looking at the little boy while continuing to toss the ball in the air.

The child remained quiet for several moments before finally saying, "I'm Colby."

"Well, hello, Colby." Keylan tossed his ball again, keeping his eyes on Colby. "How old are you?"

The little boy held up four fingers.

"He doesn't talk much. He's shy," one of the older boys said.

Keylan caught his ball and sat up. "I see," he replied before turning to face Colby. "Would you like to play a game? Maybe we can all play a game." His eyes scanned the faces of the other children.

All the other kids stopped tossing their balls, sat up and gave Keylan their undivided attention. Coach Hooper came over and stood next to the seated children. "What do you have in mind, KJ?" she asked.

Keylan looked at the kids' curious faces and smiled. "Do you guys know how to play basketball?"

Two of the older boys began rapidly nodding like bobblehead dolls as they raised their hands, singing "I do, I do…" as they jumped up and down.

"Wait a minute. Sit back down, please," Keylan said.

"Excuse me, KJ, but I'm not sure these kids are ready—"

"Of course they are, for what I have in mind. Trust me." Keylan gave her a confident smile. "Now, you two—James and David, right?" he asked, hoping he had remembered their names correctly.

They both nodded. "Yep, I'm David."

"I'm James."

"Okay, you two will be my assistants." Both boys clapped. Keylan looked up at Coach Hooper. "I hope you don't mind a little extra assistance?"

Coach Hooper laughed. "Not at all."

One of the girls said she wanted to be the cheerleader, while the other two girls insisted that they play. Keylan assured everyone that they could take any role they liked. He turned to Colby. "Do you want to play?"

Before he could respond James said, "He don't like to play with us...him too little."

"He like to play by himself," David added.

Keylan watched as Colby's eyes scanned the faces of the other kids. He figured Colby was looking for some sort of encouragement from them. "Thank you, boys, but I think he's just the right size and, if we ask him to play, he just might do it. What do you guys think?" Keylan asked, wanting the group to show some support. Some nodded and others shrugged.

"I happen to think Colby can handle anything you have in mind," Coach Hooper offered.

"See, Colby, we all think you should play. So, do you want to try? It's real easy," Keylan promised. Colby nodded his head slowly as if he really wasn't sure. "That's great."

Keylan stood and all the kids looked up at him in awe; his height really appeared to fascinate them. He was only happy no one seemed afraid of him. Not even Colby, who was now standing mere inches from him, which, for reasons he couldn't explain, made Keylan smile.

"Coach Hooper, can you please get us five basketballs and three large tubs?"

"Sure." She walked away with a confused look on her face.

"David, James, can you two please give Coach Hooper a hand?"

Both boys jumped up and ran behind Coach Hooper.

Keylan turned to the little cheerleader who was standing, practicing, and asked, "You sure you don't want to play?"

"I'm sure," she sang, shaking her imaginary pompoms.

David and James returned, both holding one side of a big blue tub with two basketballs inside. Coach Hooper was following behind them, holding the other two tubs. Keylan ran to offer assistance. The three tubs were placed in the center of the court ten feet apart. Keylan lined up three children in front of each bucket, approximately forty feet away from the bucket. Colby stood at the front of his line.

"Here's what you're going to do. Wait, how many of you know how to dribble a basketball? Hold up your hands." Every hand flew up except Colby's. "With one hand," Keylan specified, bouncing the ball with his right hand.

Several hands lowered.

"Okay, everyone put your hands down. Before we do anything, I want you to practice dribbling." He held a basketball in his left hand and raised his right. "You'll use your fingertips to control the ball as you bounce it." Keylan walked around, showing each child his technique.

"Nice job," Coach Hooper cheered.

Keylan looked over his shoulders. "Thanks, Coach Hooper. I've done this a time or two. Do you have a whistle I can borrow?"

"Sure, you can have mine," she offered, smiling as she removed the whistle that hung around her neck and handed it to him.

"Thank you," he said. The corner of his mouth rose. Keylan was just as excited about the game he was about to teach the kids as he would be when he played himself. "Please toss me a couple more basketballs."

Keylan caught the additional balls before turning his attention back to the kids. "Now, you'll all practice dribbling…" he started to explain as he handed each child at the head of the line a ball "…until you hear me blow the whistle. When you do, pass the ball to the person behind you so everyone will have a chance to practice. Everyone understand?"

"Yes," they all said in unison.

"Ready." Keylan blew the whistle. "Go."

The first three children started bouncing their balls, two with their right hand and one with his left. Keylan smiled as he walked up to each child, offering assistance on their form.

Colby was the only one that didn't need assistance; his focus and ball handling surprised Keylan. But the bigger surprise was the connection he'd made with the child. He wasn't sure what it was exactly but he knew there was something special about the boy. "Good job, Colby." The boy smiled but kept his eyes on the ball as he continued to bounce it. After two rounds of practice, Keylan blew his whistle.

"Looks like we're ready to go. Here's how the game is played." Keylan picked up a ball and demonstrated. "You'll dribble the ball down to the tubs. Go as fast as you can while controlling it. Circle the tub and dribble back. Hand the ball to the next person in line and they'll do the same. The first team back wins. Does everyone understand?"

"Yes," all the kids replied—everyone except Colby.

"Here we go." Keylan brought the whistle to his mouth.

"My team will win," the boy declared loudly and with a confident smile.

Mia sat at her desk, staring at the computer screen, reading the same paragraph she'd read three times within the last forty-five minutes and still couldn't comprehend. Her mind kept traveling to the extremely sexy but annoying man with his perfectly trimmed goatee and a smile that did crazy things to her body. She shook her head. Mia still couldn't believe she had been so rude to the boss's nephew. "Stop it." Mia removed her eyeglasses, placed them on the desk and rubbed her eyes.

"Talking to yourself again, boss lady?" Sandra asked, walking into the office carrying two large cups of tea. "Time for a break…sweet tea with lemon." She handed Mia a cup and a straw.

"Thanks, and I told you to stop calling me that," she reminded, accepting the drink. Mia placed the straw in the cup and took a big pull. "Mmm, that's good."

Sandra took one of the seats in front of her desk. "So…" She took a drink of her tea, staring at Mia.

"So what?"

"You know what. What's up with you and Mister Tall, Sexy and I'd Do Anything He Wants?" she asked, her eyebrows dancing.

Mia scowled. "Nothing's up. He's here for community service hours. That's it."

"If you ask me—"

"I didn't," she said, placing her tea on a coaster near her computer. "Now, where are we with finalizing the contract with the toy company? Their commitment to donating a hundred bikes is a critical part of our giveaway."

"Okay, I'll drop it, but you'll have to tell me where we are with the contract."

"Excuse me?" Mia's brows snapped together.

"You're the one still reviewing the contract," she noted, pointing at Mia's computer.

"Oh…" Mia glanced over her shoulder and looked at her computer. *Is that what that is?* "I guess I forgot."

"I bet you did." Sandra smirked and drained the last of her drink. "I'll wait." She placed her empty cup on the edge of Mia's desk and sat back with her arms folded.

Mia turned to fully face her computer. She put her glasses on and quickly read through the paragraphs on the screen. "Looks good." Mia hit a few keys before pushing the send button. "I just sent the electronically signed version back to you. Please send it out right away."

"I'm on it, boss lady." Mia glared at her. "Sorry." Sandra stood, picked up her cup and turned to leave.

"Sandra, can you wait a minute?" Mia removed her glasses. She picked up her pen and started tapping it on the top of her desk.

Sandra stood in front of Mia's desk. "What's up?"

"Do you know how things are going?"

Sandra frowned. "With what?"

"You know what—Keylan and Coach Wanda's class."

Sandra's frown deepened. "KJ's not with Coach Wanda's class. He's with Coach Hooper's class in the small gym. He's helping out with ball time."

"What!" Mia yelled, getting to her feet. She rounded her desk, heading out the door and down the hall.

Chapter 3

Mia stood just inside the doorway of the small gym, blinking to clear tears from her eyes. She wasn't sure if what she was seeing and hearing was real. "What's up?" Sandra asked, trying to catch her breath. "You ran out of the office so fast, I—"

Mia held up her index finger to stop her friend from speaking. Sandra turned toward the sounds and sights that held Mia's attention. "Are they playing some kind of basketball game?" she asked, her eyebrows standing at attention.

"Looks that way," Mia replied, slowly nodding. "Colby is actually talking to the other children."

"Talking? It looks like he's cheering his team on. I thought Coach Hooper said these guys weren't ready for organized sports yet."

"She did. I guess she was wrong…so was I, for that matter," Mia admitted.

"Yes!" both women screamed, jumping up and down as they watched the last child on Colby's team finish the task before anyone else, winning the game. Everyone cheered with excitement, even those children who were not on the winning team. Mia and Sandra walked over to where the children had gathered around Keylan. Sandra started giving high-fives to all the children. "That was great, you guys," Mia said, smiling at all the excited faces staring up at her.

Colby ran over to Mia and threw his arms around her waist. "Mommy, I won."

Mia knelt down and gave Colby a big hug as she fought back a fresh batch of tears. "I see that." She kissed him on the forehead. "I'm so proud of my little man."

Colby gave his mother another hug and a toothy grin before returning to his friends, who were now standing next to Coach Hooper and Sandra. "So Colby's *your* son."

Mia rose, wiped at her tears and looked up at Keylan. "Yes, he is."

Keylan stood with his feet slightly apart, rolling a basketball between his hands. "What are you doing with these kids?"

"Playing basketball." Keylan looked over his shoulder at the kids, who were now dribbling balls all over the court, and smirked. "Our version of it, anyway. Colby…that's a great kid you got there."

"Thank you." Mia wrapped her arms around her waist. It was either a protective gesture or a nervous habit that she'd given up trying to break a long time ago. Keylan's kind words and the excitement radiating from his body at playing with the kids had her heart doing flips. Not to mention the way the rest of her body was responding to his nearness. "You were supposed to be helping with the older kids."

"I know, but when I passed by this gym and saw these guys, something drew me in."

"They can have that effect on people," she said, smiling.

Keylan gave Mia a half smile. "Do you mind if I—?"

"Key…lan," Colby sang. "Key…lan."

"Looks like I'm being summoned. Can we pick this up later when I'm done?"

"Key...lan," Colby yelled, jumping up and down.

Mia's eyes widened. She had never seen her son respond to anything or anyone in such a way.

"Demanding little dude. I guess he gets it from you," he said with a sneer.

"He's usually shy around strangers. Loud noises, inanimate objects that move or too much commotion makes him nervous...freaks him out." Mia wondered if she looked as confused as she felt.

"Maybe it's just me. Until later," Keylan called over his shoulder, returning to Colby and the other children.

"Looks like Colby's made a big new friend," Sandra said, coming to stand next to Mia.

"Yeah, and that's what I'm afraid of," Mia replied, her forehead creased.

Keylan had showered, changed into his street clothes and was sitting on the bench in front of his locker, flipping through his phone messages, but found his ability to concentrate fleeting. He was still flying high from all the fun he'd had hanging with all those kids today, especially Colby. The way Colby seemed to come alive around him made his heart swell. His brilliant and very beautiful mother was making him crazy in ways no other woman had and that scared the hell out of him. All he could think about was Mia's short but athletic legs, her small waist and ample breasts. Keylan had been so deep in thought that he didn't hear his name being called. "KJ," a raised baritone voice said before a quick punch landed on Keylan's right shoulder. He looked up to find his cousin Travis smiling down at him.

Travis Kingsley looked like a fairer-skinned version of Keylan. A wildly successful cattle rancher, he was the only son of Keylan's aunt Elizabeth. Travis served as Chairman of the Board of Directors for the family's foundation.

"You don't want none of this, son," Keylan replied, laughing, placing his phone down on the bench before the two men bumped fists.

"What are you doing here and what has you so engrossed in thought that you didn't hear me coming? You know what Aunt Victoria always says," Travis prompted.

"Always be aware of your surroundings," they said in unison.

Keylan nodded. "How can I forget? She only drilled it in our heads for years." The two men were more like brothers than cousins. After all, they'd all been raised together.

"So what's going on? I hear you were working with our Down's kids," Travis asked. "I know how special that group is to you."

"Yeah, they're a really great bunch of kids. I had no idea we'd doubled our initial admission numbers."

"I know, and while I appreciate you finally making time to stop by, I can't help but wonder what prompted this visit, especially while you're in the middle of your rehab." Travis leaned against the locker, crossed his arms at his chest and his feet at the ankles.

"I can't believe the story hasn't been picked up by the media yet." Keylan grabbed his phone and searched his name online. "Yep, it's there."

"What's there?"

Keylan handed Travis his phone. He preferred for his cousin to read the articles for himself. "Man, that's BS. Z's reaction to that play was a flop. Everyone knows he made that fall look worse than it really was. Now you get suspended for three games, along with having to pay a fine *and* perform community service because of his punk-ass move."

"I really don't mind doing the service or paying the

fine. Hell, I'll even accept the three-game suspension, although I do find it excessive, especially since it won't be imposed until next season. It's being labeled a selfish bully on the court. I may be aggressive when I play, but I'm no selfish bully."

"Since when do you give a damn about what people think?"

"Since now," Keylan said, accepting his phone back from Travis.

"Now I see why you were so deep in thought when I came up. But there's no better place to get your hours completed than in a place you help build and financially support."

"Tell that to our activities director." Keylan sat his phone on the bench next to his keys.

"Mia?" Travis's eyes widened and he stood straight.

"She thinks I'm a rich and overprivileged playboy."

Travis grimaced. "Well…"

"Okay, but she also thinks I'm only here going through the motions."

"That's because she doesn't know your history here or the fact that you paid for that massive gym with your NBA money. I guess you failed to mention those facts." Travis smiled. "She's good people. I wouldn't worry about it."

Keylan rose from the bench and placed his hands in his pockets. "Why the defense…she yours or something?"

A smile crawled across Travis's face as he stood in silence for a moment. "Why? You interested or something?"

Keylan and his cousin had always been competitive when it came to sports and sometimes business, but never when it came to women. Blood was blood. As much as it bothered Keylan to lie to his cousin, if Travis had a thing for Mia, he would never know how much Keylan was attracted to her, too.

"You know she's not my type…too short. Plus, she has a kid. I don't date women with kids, although Colby really is cute and could use some KJs or at least some Jordans in his life. Those Velcro things she's got on his feet are ridiculous."

Travis gave Keylan a lopsided grin. "What?"

"You *do* like her." Travis burst out laughing, slowly clapping his hands.

Keylan reached down and picked up his phone and keys. "I didn't say that."

"You didn't have to."

"Well…" Keylan said, trying but failing to look disinterested.

"Well, what?" Travis teased. Keylan glared at him. "No man, Mia is great, but she's my friend and our employee. That's all."

"Really?"

"Really. But heed my warning—Mia's not one to be toyed with," Travis warned.

"I'm not looking to toy with anyone. Besides, she's not—"

"Your type, so you've said. I'm not buying it."

"If she's so great, why didn't you asked her out? Or have you? What, she turn you down?" Keylan laughed.

"She's our employee, so no, I haven't asked her out. If you're not interested, why all the questions?"

Good question.

While Mia wasn't the type of woman Keylan usually went for—tall, agreeable and strictly fun—the idea of Mia and Travis together annoyed the hell out of him. Keylan's phone beeped and he was relieved by the interruption. He read his text. "What's up with my mom? She's texted me like ten times within the last thirty minutes."

"She's trying to confirm that you'll be at the dinner meeting she scheduled tonight."

"Why, what's going on?"

"I don't know, but it must be something big, because she sent James to give me a personal invite since I didn't answer her twenty text messages."

Keylan shook his head. "Man, my mother is something else. I'm surprised James hasn't quit with all the crazy errands she makes him run."

"James quit? Never. He's been Aunt Victoria's personal assistant since your dad died." Travis's forehead creased. "Did you ever wonder if he and your mom—?"

"Hell no," Keylan admitted, shivering at the thought. "I wouldn't want to know, either."

"Me, either. Just send her a text and let her know you'll be there tonight."

Keylan sighed and obliged. "I swear, if this ends up being another one of her 'When are you going to settle down and give me grandbabies?' speeches, I'm going to get up and leave. It's not like she's the warm-and-fuzzy-grandmother type who wants grandkids she can boast about and hang out with. All she's concerned about is having heirs to carry on her legacy."

"So, back to you and Mia."

A beautiful, sassy and very sexy woman with a really cool kid is the last thing I need in my life right now. "There is no me and Mia," Keylan said, heading for the exit.

Chapter 4

Mia walked through the door of her three-bedroom bungalow behind her son, holding two bags of groceries and her son's backpack. They walked through the living and dining room, passing an oversize, brown stress-leather sofa and a large bay window with a wide bench, to get to her grand, black-and-white gourmet kitchen that sat off her family room. "Good job, little man. Now place the milk on the table and go put your backpack away."

"I no have it," he replied, frowning, showing Mia his empty hands.

Mia smiled. "It's by the front door. I dropped it next to Mommy's purse."

"Okeydoke," he sang, running out of the kitchen.

Mia placed the grocery bags on her kitchen island. She looked around the room and her smile widened. Mia still couldn't believe how great her remodel had turned out, especially after she'd fired her initial contractor for the rude remarks he'd continuously made about her son.

"Backpack's up, Mommy. Colby big boy."

"I know," she confirmed as she put away her groceries. "How about beans, wieners and a salad for dinner?"

"No salad." His face scrunched up.

"Yes, a little salad."

"Call Keylan now?" he asked, jumping up and down.

"Colby, we talked about this already, son. Keylan is very busy right now."

"I want to talk to Keylan now," he insisted, his little hands fisted at his sides.

Mia sighed. "Mommy doesn't have his number." Colby ran from the room. "I guess I'm not winning Mommy of the Year again." Mia looked over at the last award Colby had made for her that still hung on the information board in their kitchen.

Colby ran back into the kitchen, smiling. "I got it."

"Got what?" she asked, her back turned away from her son as she opened the can of beans, pouring them into a small pot before she lit the fire on her gas stove under the pan.

"Keylan's number."

Mia turned around so fast she nearly gave them both whiplash. "What?"

"Keylan's number," he said, waving a business card in the air.

Mia took the card and read the handwritten message on the back. *Call me anytime, little man.* "Great," she snapped.

Colby ran out of the kitchen again, only to return seconds later holding his mother's cell phone. "Call Keylan."

Mia exhaled noisily and turned on the fire under the pan of hot dogs. She accepted the phone, looked at the number and started dialing.

Please don't answer...please don't answer.

Keylan had just pulled his black Sienna Porsche into the large circular driveway of his aunt's mini mansion when his phone rang. He looked at the number but didn't recognize it. Since only a handful of people had his private number, he answered it.

"Keylan Kingsley."

"Hello, Mr. Kingsley." Keylan knew instantly who it was. The edge to her voice was very familiar.

"It's Keylan or KJ, Mia," he reminded her.

"You gave my son your business card."

Keylan didn't know if that was a statement or a question. He decided on the former. "I know. And I told him to call me whenever he wanted."

"I really hope you're not using my son to get to me because that would not only be despicable, but a waste of time."

"My, my, aren't we full of ourselves. Is it so hard to believe I could actually like your son, see something pretty special about him?"

"Well—"

"And, for the record, when I want a woman, I go to her. I don't need to use anyone," he said, trying to control his annoyance.

"I wanna talk to Keylan!" he heard the boy say in the background.

"May I speak with Colby, please?"

"Yes, of course. One moment please." Her tone turned pleasant.

"Hi, Keylan!"

"Hello, buddy. How are you?"

"I'm fine."

"What are you doing?" Keylan was excited to hear Colby's voice and curious about his answer.

"I'm talking to you."

Keylan laughed. "Yes, you are. Did you want to tell or ask me something?"

"Come play with me tomorrow. I'll be good. I promise!"

Keylan's heart flipped. "Yes, buddy, I'll come play with you tomorrow. I promise."

"Okay..."

"I'll see you tomorrow." Keylan listened for a response but the phone fell silent. "I guess that's that."

Keylan put his phone in his pocket and exited the car. He made his way to his aunt Elizabeth's front door. It always made him laugh, entering her mustard-color house through a bright white door. Keylan had raised his hand to knock when the door opened. Elizabeth Kingsley, his mother's sister and only sibling, had raised her children alongside his mother's after both their husbands had been killed in a plane crash.

"There's my tall, handsome nephew," Elizabeth said, pulling him into her outstretched arms.

"You say that about all of your nephews." He stepped out of her arms and kissed her on the cheek. "Now, don't you look sunny?" Keylan smiled, admiring the bright green, short-sleeved dress she wore with no shoes. Her wrinkle-free, fair skin, makeup-free, only accentuated her youthful image. Her shoulder-length, dark brown hair was pulled up into a ponytail. She looked nowhere near her fifty-two years.

"I know. Now, get in here. Everyone's dining already. Your mother is losing her mind."

They walked halfway down her white-marble hall and turned right into a large, bright, circular dining room with walls of gold leaf. His mother and cousin were seated at the large, sixteen-seat table that dominated the room.

"This is everyone?" With six kids in the family, Keylan wasn't used to such a small gathering whenever his mother and aunt required their presences for dinner. "Where is everyone else?"

"This business dinner isn't for everyone, just you and Travis."

"Look who finally showed up." Victoria Kingsley stood

and crossed her arms. "Did *all* your time-keeping mechanisms fail you, son?" she asked, sarcastically glancing at his watch.

"Good to see you, too, Mother." Keylan kissed her on both cheeks.

Victoria Kingsley, a tall, more slender version of her sister, the powerful matriarch of her family, looked more like someone's thirty-year-old sister than a fifty-four-year-old mother of four adult men. The no-nonsense business-woman could even be ruthless at times.

"Enough of the pleasantries, let's get down to business." Victoria sat at the table where several documents and a laptop were placed. Elizabeth sat next to her. Keylan sat across from his cousin.

"Victoria, can you at least wait until the dinner is on the table?" Elizabeth pleaded.

Victoria heaved a sigh, reached for the glass of wine in front of her and sat back in her chair. "Thank you. It'll only take a few more minutes. You flew in here so fast, barking orders, I didn't get to ask about the highlight of your day." Elizabeth smiled like an excited child.

"This should be good," Keylan interjected.

"Man, don't start," Travis said, shaking his head.

"Of course, just as long as you stick to the rules." Elizabeth smiled. "Positives only, please."

When Victoria and Elizabeth had been forced to raise their children alone and run their growing businesses together, they'd had to make several adjustments to their daily routine and find creative ways to make sure the relatives all remained close as possible. One way they'd done that was by sharing their daily highs and lows over nightly dinner.

Victoria returned her sister's smile and placed her wine-glass on the table. "This is my highlight. Seeing the son and nephew I don't see nearly enough because they chose not to come work for our family business." Victoria picked up her glass and raised it in the air as if she had just made a toast.

Elizabeth threw her head back and laughed. "You really can't help yourself, can you? Well, it seems we share the same highlight, only for different reasons."

"Surprise…surprise." Victoria took a drink.

Travis raised his right hand. "I'll go next. My highlight was seeing Romeo over there—" he pointed to Keylan "—tripping all over himself behind Mia."

"Mia?" his mother and aunt echoed.

Keylan narrowed his eyes at his cousin before turning his attention back to the choir of two. "I was not tripping over Mia. I've never met her before and I think she has a really cool kid, is all." Keylan picked up a glass of water and drank it down like he was a man just escaping the desert.

Travis smirked. "Yeah, she's fine as hell, but one hard nut to crack."

Keylan put down his empty glass a little harder than he intended. "What did you just say?" he demanded, feeling unexpected anger building inside him.

Travis jumped up, started laughing and clapping. "Told you. I *told* you."

"Travis, behave yourself and stop teasing your cousin," Elizabeth ordered, smiling. She'd always felt her and Victoria's children were more like siblings than cousins.

"I can't believe you fell for that, son." Victoria shook her head as she took another sip of her wine.

Linda, Elizabeth's longtime housekeeper, entered the room, rolling her service cart. She placed a plate with lamb chops, potatoes and greens in front of everyone before making her exit. Everyone bowed their head as Victoria blessed the food. "Now that the dinner has been served, can I please get back to my agenda?" Victoria asked her sister.

"Not yet. We obviously know Travis's highlight of the day but I don't know Keylan's." Elizabeth smiled.

Victoria sat back in her chair and raised her hands in surrender.

Keylan, who was now cutting his meat, could see the excitement and expectation on his aunt's face. He could even see the interest in his mother's eyes that she was trying to hide. He looked over at his cousin, who was waiting to pounce, and placed his knife and fork down.

"Yes, my highlight was meeting a really cool kid and his interesting mother." Keylan turned to his cousin. "Happy?"

"Yep," Travis acknowledged, placing a piece of meat in his mouth.

"Now may I continue?" Victoria asked to no one in particular.

"Of course." Elizabeth began to dig into her food.

"The rest of the family already knows this, but we're about to go to war with the Occupational Safety and Health Administration and the IRS!"

Chapter 5

Mia walked into her son's bedroom and smiled at all the superheroes that greeted her entrance. A poster featuring all his favorite characters had been placed on the right wall where his bed sat. The round rug covered a large portion of the dark hardwood floor and a beanbag chair sat next to the window. Mia walked to the left side of the room and placed Colby's laundry in his dresser drawers. She crossed the room to turn down the comforter when she heard her son running down the hall.

Colby ran into the room wearing his superhero pj's and jumped on his bed. "Teeth all clean! See, Mommy?" He opened his mouth wide.

"I see. Good job."

"Story time…" Colby leaped off the bed and went to select a book from the shelf under his window.

"Cat hat book," he said, climbing back on the bed and handing it to Mia.

"It's *The Cat in the Hat*, Colby," she replied, accepting the book, kissing him on the head. "Under the covers you go."

"Mommy, Keylan is coming tomorrow," he said, smiling.

Mia's heart jumped at the thought of seeing Keylan

again. She sat next to her son on the bed. "Is he, now?" she said, opening the book.

"Yep. I can't wait."

"That's great, son. Now, let's start the story."

Mia expected she'd have to read the book a few times before Colby fell asleep. He always found reasons to stay up past his bedtime. However, it seemed his excitement to see Keylan outweighed his need to stay awake. She kissed her sleeping son, put the book away and pulled his door closed, leaving it cracked open.

She made her way back to the kitchen, where she pulled out a bottle of Stella Rosa from the refrigerator and poured herself a glass. She took a sip before she started to clean the kitchen.

Mia had just finished loading the dinner dishes into the dishwasher when her cell phone rang. She looked at her phone and smiled. "Aunt Mavis, is everything all right?" Mia, born to a teenage mother who'd decided after few years that parenthood wasn't for her, had been raised by her mother's sister and her husband. She often found it ironic that she too had become a single mother; only she couldn't imagine not raising her son.

"Of course it is. I was just checking in to see how my favorite niece and great-nephew are doing."

Mia laughed. "We're fine. Just as fine as we were when you called yesterday."

"Well, a lot can happen in twenty-four hours," she said matter-of-factly.

"You're right. How's Uncle Rudy?"

"He's good for a seventy-five-year-old man," she said, and offered a hearty laugh. "Have you thought about our gift?"

Mia heaved a sigh as she turned on the dishwasher. Topping off her wineglass before returning the bottle to the refrigerator, she turned off the lights and headed to her bedroom, making a brief detour to look in on her son.

"Auntie, we discussed this already." She sat on her bed, took a drink from her glass before setting it on her nightstand. "I really appreciate the offer, but Colby and I won't be joining you on your cruise."

"I don't understand why not. It's not like you celebrate Christmas in a big fashion, anyway. Why not join us for an adventure on the sea? Lord knows you have the vacation days and you certainly could use an adventure."

Mia could hear the irritation in her aunt's voice at her unwillingness to take time off from work and have a little fun as she was always advising her to do. "First, it's your fiftieth wedding anniversary, and second, it's your fiftieth wedding anniversary."

"It's not like I'm asking you to share our cabin. Like you said, it is our anniversary and we need our privacy."

"Eww…"

"Eww, child, you better pray you find a man where everything works at seventy-five except his hearing. He don't have to hear to know what I need," she said, laughing.

"TMI, Auntie."

"Speaking of men…"

"We weren't speaking of men, Auntie." Mia took a sip of her wine.

"Well, we are now. You remember Curly Ellis, right? Well, he has a son that's single—"

"Please don't. I'm not looking—"

"Sometimes you don't have a choice in the matter. Your heart makes the choice for you."

"Yeah, we see how well that turned out last time," she murmured.

"Yes, we do. You got a beautiful and very special son

out the deal. It's not your fault his father didn't realize what gems he had in you two."

Mia felt tears fill her eyes because she knew her aunt was right. Her ex, Louis, might have been an ass about the situation, but she had her son and a support system in her aunt and uncle that brought nothing but love and laughter to her life. While she'd often wondered what life would have been like, married to an NBA player and having a partner to help raise her son, she had never once regretted her decision to go it alone.

"You're so right, Auntie, so why mess with a good thing?"

"Because Colby will grow into an independent young man who won't want his spinster mother hanging around cramping his style."

"Ouch…"

"I'm just keeping it real, as you young folks say. Besides, you need someone to love you the way you deserve to be loved, and Colby needs a father. Not a seventy-five-year-old father figure that can't hear too good."

"Uncle Rudy is great." Mia ran her hand through her hair.

"I know he is and he's mine. You need your own Rudy."

"There aren't too many like Uncle Rudy out there—plus, I'm scared of Colby getting hurt."

"You mean you're scared to get hurt again. Kids are resilient. Especially Colby. He's already had to deal with so much in his young life, and he just keeps on keeping on. I just wish he'd come out of his shell more with people other than us."

"Actually—"

"Actually…what?"

"He's taken to talking to one of our volunteers." Mia hoped her aunt would let it go at that but she knew better.

"Oh. Who?"

"Elizabeth Kingsley's nephew, the NBA star."

"KJ?" Mavis's voice escalated.

"You know who he is?"

"Your uncle was a basketball coach with the school system for thirty years, remember?"

"Of course I remember. Well, they seem to have developed some kind of bond."

"Hmm…"

"Hmm…what?"

"He's single, right?" Mia could imagine all the thoughts flying through her aunt's mind.

"I guess, if you mean he's not married. Men like him are rarely single."

"There you go again, generalizing." It was a criticism Mavis had often leveled at Mia. "Not all professional athletes are butts like Louis. He just might prove you wrong. After all, you'll be spending time with him—"

"Auntie, I told you—"

"And I told *you*." The phone fell silent for several moments. "You like him."

Mia pushed out a breath. "He's all right."

"I knew it." Mia heard her aunt clapping. "Looks like your heart beat me to the punch."

"Wait a minute. Yes, I think he's attractive, but I also think he's an arrogant playboy who dates leggy models and would have no interest in a package deal."

"You'll never know unless you ask."

"No, thank you. Now, I'm going to go get ready for tomorrow. Thanks again for the vacation offer, but we'll be just fine spending Christmas at home."

"You'll at least attend church, right?" Her aunt's voice was stern.

"Just like always."

"Okay, I'll drop it…for now. Good night, beautiful one."

"Back at you, Auntie."

"What? We just got through dealing with the EPA," Keylan proclaimed.

"I realize that, son," Victoria replied, her irritation coming through loud and clear. "However, OSHA will soon be sending someone to investigate claims of worksite violations, and the IRS is moving up our annual audit."

"That's ridiculous," Travis snarled.

"Be that as it may, we need to be prepared for another onset of bad press heading our way—and we don't need any more," she declared, leveling her attention on her son.

"What?" Keylan replied.

"You know what, Mr. Headline Grabber." Victoria reached for her wineglass and took a sip.

"It's not Keylan's fault that the press likes to pick on him." Elizabeth defended him.

Victoria looked at her sister and scrunched up her face.

"Thank you, Aunt Elizabeth." Keylan smiled and winked at her while Travis rolled his eyes at the exchange.

"Oh, please, sis, stop coddling the boy—excuse me, the man." Victoria turned her attention back to her son. "Don't give the press anything else to write about. Between your suspension and now these new claims, we have enough to deal with."

"What?" Elizabeth frowned and placed both hands over her heart. "Keylan, you were suspended?"

"Yes. Me and this other player were both playing pretty aggressively all night when we collided in the air when we were both going for the rebound. I landed pretty hard on top of him."

"Well, accidents happen." Elizabeth frowned.

"I know, Aunt Elizabeth, but according to the league, they thought I purposely came down hard on him."

"It was a BS charge, too," Travis offered.

"Thanks, cousin."

"Victoria…" Elizabeth glared at her sister.

Keylan knew his aunt would expect his mother to fix his situation. She thought her sister could do anything and, usually, she could. However, not even the great Victoria Kingsley could make this go away.

"Don't 'Victoria' me—talk to your favorite nephew."

Keylan smiled, because no matter how much she loved all her nephews or how hard she tried to deny it, he knew his aunt had taken a special liking to him. "Don't worry about it, Aunt Elizabeth. It's only three games after I'm released to play again and eighty hours of community service. Everything will be fine. Don't worry about it."

"Now, back to the subject at hand. I need everyone on their best behavior," Victoria stated.

"That includes you, too, son." Elizabeth smirked.

"Mom, you know I stay as far away from the media as I can get."

"Yes, you do, but that won't stop them from coming for you, so just be alert and stay careful."

"Yes, ma'am," Travis said.

"Keylan, darling, I'm going to be helping out at the office a little more, so I need for you to pick up the slack at the foundation. You're going to be there anyway. Might as well make yourself useful." Victoria's eyes lased in on her sister.

"Well, I—"

"You what, son?" Her eyes bored into him. "Elizabeth's right. You *will* be spending a great deal of time at our foundation, and I'm sure you have a few ideas about how we can expand the services we provide. Aren't you the one always telling us we should do this and that to make the foundation better? Well, now's your chance. Be the change you seek. Anyway, you'll have Mia there to help you."

"I'm sure she'll be very helpful," he declared sarcastically, trying to ignore the instant and relentless attraction he was feeling toward her.

Chapter 6

Mia pulled her gray Range Rover Sport, a splurge she'd allowed herself to take with her last holiday bonus, into her assigned parking spot of the Kingsley Foundation building. Parked in the executive space was a black Porsche; Mia knew who it had to belong to and her heart skipped several beats.

"Oh, no…"

"What's wrong, Mommy?" Colby asked, frowning.

"Nothing, honey. Get your backpack. You don't want to be late."

"I'm not late. I'm going to see Keylan."

I know. Mia exited the car and helped Colby out. She ran her hand through his curly hair to clear his eyes. "You need a haircut."

"No, Mommy."

"Yes, son. Now tuck in your shirt."

Colby tucked his white foundation shirt into his dark khaki shorts, put on his backpack and, with his head down, made his way up the walkway toward the door. "Slow down, Colby, and watch where you're going."

Ignoring his mother, Colby opened the front door and took off down the hall, heading to his class. Mia walked through the door in time to see Colby run directly into Keylan, who caught him before he hit the ground. "Whoa, slow down, little man, and watch where you're going. Men, big and small, always walk with their heads held high. It commands respect and it shows confidence," Keylan educated his young new friend.

"Colby, baby," Mia called out, running to her son's side. "Are you okay?"

"I'm fine, Mommy." His voice was stern and his chin rose. Mia knew how much he hated being treated like a baby.

Mia looked up at Keylan and offered him a half smile. "Sorry about that. He's a little excited to get here today. You have to watch where you're going, Colby. We talked about this," she scolded.

"What's confidence, Mommy?" Mia cut her eyes to Keylan before dropping them back to her son.

"It means you believe in yourself, in what you can do," she explained.

"I'm confidence I can play with Keylan today," he declared with a big smile.

Keylan grinned. "Yes, I will, but *after* school."

"No, play now." Colby stomped his foot and fisted his hands at his sides. Mia knew a full-blown tantrum would soon follow. It was something she rarely experienced and it was usually done in private.

"Colby—"

Keylan raised his hand to stop Mia's intervention, knelt and held Colby's gaze. "No," he replied with a little more bass in his voice. "I said we'll play after school. School first and, if you're good…" Keylan gave a half smile as if he was prompting Colby.

Colby sighed, dropped his little shoulders and relaxed his hands. "I get to play with Keylan."

"That's right." His voice had returned to its normal octave. Keylan ran his hand through Colby's hair. "You need a haircut, little man."

"Keylan can cut it." Colby's eyebrows stood at attention.

"Sure—"

Mia cleared her throat. "Time to get to class, son."

Keylan stood. "See you later, man."

"Bye, Keylan," Colby called as he made his way down the hall toward his teacher, who was waving and greeting him with a friendly smile.

"Bye, son," Mia whispered, suddenly feeling like a third wheel.

"I am—"

"I would appreciate it if you wouldn't try to discipline my son." Mia moved past Keylan and walked toward her office. *The nerve of him.*

"Good morning," Sandra greeted, her eyes scanning Mia's outfit: a Michael Kors camouflage short-sleeved scoop-necked dress and platform heels. "Where are you going?"

"Morning," Mia replied, ignoring her question, walking into her office with Keylan on her heels.

Keylan crossed the office threshold and closed the door behind him. "Excuse me."

Mia set her things on her desk and turned to face Keylan, her hands placed firmly on her hips. "You heard me. I'm perfectly capable of handling my son's inappropriate behavior. I don't need your help."

Keylan slowly walked toward Mia. She couldn't help but notice how handsome he looked in his blue suit and she wanted to kick herself. "I wasn't disciplining Colby. Discipline indicates some form of punishment has been imposed. What I did was simply educate him on a few facts about our male species and remind Colby of our deal, which allowed him to self-correct."

Mia wrapped her arms around her waist and raised her chin slightly. "I could've handled it." She knew she was overreacting but Colby's growing infatuation with Keylan annoyed her.

"I'm sure you could have," he said. The corners of his mouth rose slightly.

"What are you doing here so early?"

"My aunt Elizabeth asked me to cover a few things here for her, since I'll be hanging out at the office for a few weeks."

Lucky me. "Cover things like what, if you don't mind my asking?"

"Not at all. There are a couple of meetings she'd like me to take and I have a few ideas regarding some new programs and activities we'd like to explore."

"New activities?"

There was a knock on the door and it opened slowly. "Good morning," a soft voice called out.

Mia dropped her arms and took a step forward. "Miss Elizabeth, good morning."

"Good morning, Mia, darling," she replied, pulling her into a hug.

"Aunt Elizabeth, you're early." Keylan hugged his aunt and kissed her on the cheek. "You look lovely."

Elizabeth looked down at her gray, pleated, short-sleeved Calvin Klein dress and smiled. "Thank you. Your mother insisted that I dress a little more conservative when I come into the office. But—" she pointed to her gray-and-hot-pink shoes with bows on the heels "—she can't control everything." She laughed.

Mia smiled and Keylan laughed. "She certainly tries. Good for you, Auntie."

"Can I get you anything to drink? Tea perhaps?" Mia offered.

Elizabeth took a seat in one of the chairs facing Mia's desk. Mia sat in the one next to hers while Keylan stood beside the desk, his hands in his pockets.

"No, I've had my fill. I just wanted to bring you up to date on a decision we've made."

Mia's eyes cut to Keylan's. "Yes, your nephew was just bringing me up to speed on things."

"With our company coming under siege by the government, my sister needs me to play a more active role. I do own half the company." She crossed her legs at her ankles and gripped her crystal-encrusted handbag. "I know it's hard to believe, but my sister has a few weaknesses that I help strengthen."

"My mother weak? Not possible," Keylan mocked.

"I must agree. Your sister's the most intimidating person I've ever met," Mia confessed.

Elizabeth laughed. "Our husbands, who were brothers, were intimidating. My sister is just about as weak as I am strong," she admitted.

"I'm sorry, but I can't believe that. You're one of the strongest people I know," Mia declared while Keylan nodded in agreement.

"Thank you, my dear, but we all have our weaknesses or weak moments. The key is finding someone who's there for us in those moments." Mia's and Keylan's eyes collided. "With the death of our husbands, we became that for each other… That's enough of that. I've asked Keylan to step in for me here so I can help Victoria. I'm leaving you in good hands."

Mia angled her body more toward Elizabeth. "With all due respect, Miss Elizabeth, and no offense—" She looked up briefly at Keylan, who was slowly shaking his head. "What does he know about the daily operations of the foundation?"

The corners of Keylan's mouth turned up as he leaned back against Mia's desk, then slowly removed his hands from his pockets and raised them. "I assure you, Mia, my hands are quite capable."

Elizabeth swatted Keylan's hand. "Stop teasing Mia. My dear, I assure you my nephew is more than capable of running this place. After all, this foundation was his idea." Elizabeth rose from her seat. "Now I'm going to go say hello to everyone before I head out. Walk with me, Keylan."

His idea?

"Of course." Keylan offered her his arm.

"Have a good day, my dear, and kiss that beautiful son of yours."

"Yes, ma'am." Mia stood and watched as the Kingsleys took their exit. She walked around her desk, plopped down in her chair and kicked off her shoes. Crossing her arms on her desk, she dropped her head down.

"Mia?" Sandra called, walking into the office. "Are you all right?"

"Not even a little bit." Mia raised her head. "Close the door."

Sandra complied and took a seat. "What's going on?"

"It seems Mr. Kingsley will be 'assisting'—" she used air quotes to emphasize the word "—us for the next I-don't-know-how-long."

Sandra presented Mia with a smile that spoke volumes. "Really?"

Mia rolled her eyes skyward. "Can you please keep your hormones in check for just a moment and focus on what that means?"

"What does that mean?" Sandra frowned.

"I don't know, and that's the problem. Get this—according to Elizabeth Kingsley the foundation was his idea."

"Seriously?"

"Yep, and since he's a Kingsley and this is their foundation, he can do whatever the heck he wants, with or without my input."

"Well, that explains all that additional equipment that just got delivered to the gym."

Mia frowned. "What equipment?"

"The treatment table, a NordicTrack, an exercise bike, an electrical muscle-stimulation machine and a bunch of rubber-band-looking things." Her confusion was clear.

"They're called isokinetics. They help build strength and assist with flexibility," Keylan explained, walking into the office.

"What's up with the electrical muscle machine?" Sandra asked, flexing her arm muscles. "I could use some help in that area but I really don't like to sweat. Unless it's sexy time and—"

"Sandra." Mia glared at her friend and assistant.

Keylan snickered. "Electrical muscle stimulation helps rebuild basic tone and strengthens. If you'd really like to work on building muscles, I can recommend a good personal trainer I know."

"He single?" Sandra's eyes lit up.

"No, *she's* married," he advised.

Sandra shrugged. "I'll think about it. Do you need anything else, boss lady?"

"Yes, I need you to stop calling me boss lady."

"Got it," she said, laughing, as she walked out of the room.

"What's going on? Why are you having all this equipment delivered here?" Mia questioned.

"I'm moving my therapy session here," he explained, silencing his buzzing phone.

"You're doing what?" Mia's eyes widened.

"It just makes sense. I'll be working here every day for

the next few weeks, so having my physical therapy here will make it that much easier to balance it all."

"About that..."

Keylan's forehead creased. "What about it?"

Before Mia could reply there was a knock on the open door. "Excuse me, but no one's at the desk," a tall and slender dark-haired beauty, wearing a pink-and-black workout outfit similar to one Mia owned—only she was sure it didn't look nearly as good on her—interrupted, smiling.

Keylan looked over his shoulder and gifted the beautiful woman with a broad smile. It was the type of smile that caused a pain in Mia's heart; one she couldn't explain. Keylan stood. "McKenzie, what're you doing here so early?" He checked his watch.

"I was in the area and since my appointment canceled, I figured I'd stop by and check out the new setup. Did everything arrive on time?"

"Sure did, thanks for setting everything up for me."

"Anything for you, you know that," she said, giving Keylan a smile so wide Mia swore she could see every tooth in her head.

Mia cleared her throat.

"My apologies, please excuse my manners. Mia, this is McKenzie, she's my—"

"Oh, yes, his personal trainer." For some reason knowing that this beautiful woman was in fact his married personal trainer made Mia feel better instantly. "Pleased to meet you. We were just talking about you." Mia offered her hand.

The woman's eyebrows rose and she gave Mia's hand a small shake. "Actually, I am—"

"Dr. McKenzie Lee, and she's not my trainer," Keylan corrected. "McKenzie's my physical therapist."

"Oh, sorry about that." Mia's eyes automatically dropped to the woman's ring-free hands.

"No problem." She turned her attention to Keylan. "Care to show me around, KJ?"

"Sure, but at breakfast you said you had another appointment."

Breakfast with a tall, beautiful doctor. I should have known. Mia had no idea why she was so annoyed by the idea.

"I did, but it got canceled, too. If you have time, we can get started early."

"Sure." Keylan turned to face Mia. "I made a few notes and recommendations on activities and programs that I'd like for you to review. I emailed them to you. We can discuss them this afternoon."

"Of course." Mia's eyes bore into him. She didn't even try to hide her annoyance.

"Until later, then..."

Chapter 7

Mia watched as Keylan led his beautiful therapist out of the office. She went back to her desk, sat down and fired up her computer. "Notes for me to review. Who the hell does he think he is? The boss, that's who," she reminded herself, sitting back in her chair, waiting for her computer to come to life.

Sandra walked into the office holding a tray with a plate of muffins and two glasses of milk. "I thought we could use a morning break so we can sample some of the new chef's muffins." She took a big whiff. "They look and smell divine."

Mia sat forward and her brows snapped together. "Wait—what new chef?"

"Her name is Donna Shea. From what I could gather, she's Keylan's personal chef and has been for years."

"So he brought in his personal chef to cook for him while he's here?" She rolled her eyes skyward. "Typical rich-playboy crap."

"No, she's here to help out. She's going to run the kitchen from now on. I guess Keylan wants to bring in some extra help for the line cooks," Sandra replied before biting into a cranberry muffin.

"Who authorized this change?"

Sandra covered her mouth and said, "He did, I guess. Anyway, the cooks don't seem to mind much." She picked up her glass and drank some of her milk. "Damn, this is good. It's made with Greek yogurt."

Remembering Keylan's final words, Mia turned to her computer, searched her system and found his email. She began reading through his notes and recommendations. "Hmm…" Mia frowned.

"What is it?" Sandra asked, reaching for one of the blueberry muffins. "You're not having one?"

Mia waved off her friend and continued reading.

"Whatever you're reading can't be as good as these muffins," Sandra said, licking her fingers.

Mia released a deep sigh. "Since I haven't tried the muffins, I can't make a comparison. However, his program recommendations and changes to the nutritional menus are actually pretty good."

"Care to share?"

"He wants to use that tract of land between the kitchen and the playground to cultivate a garden so we can grow vegetables and herbs that can be used in the kitchen. He even wants to set up cooking classes for the kids and their parents. He basically wants to help bring better eating habits to the community at large."

"Well, that's cool." Sandra finished off her milk. "You sound surprised."

"I am, actually. I wonder what other surprises he has in store for me," she said, reaching for a cranberry muffin as she continued to read. "He wants to offer more services to the community."

"Like what?"

"Extended child care. He wants to institute a parents' night out program and extend some of the financial and educational services we already offer. He's even attached relevant research to his proposal. His recommendations are actually pretty insightful."

"That all sounds great. Personally, I can't wait until lunchtime."

Mia laughed. "Why?" she asked, using her mouse to flip through the pages on her screen.

"Because Ms. Donna is making fish and turkey tacos for everyone. If they are half as good as these muffins, we're in for a real treat." Sandra stood, gathered up the trash and empty glasses. "I better get back to work."

"Yes, you should," Mia agreed, smiling up at Sandra and watching as she left the office, closing the door behind her.

Mia printed out all the documents and immediately began reading through them, making notes as she read. Halfway through, Mia found her mind drifting toward thoughts of the author. She checked her watch and was surprised to see how close to noon it had gotten.

Mia sat back in her chair and began tapping her nails on her desk. "Oh, what the hell...that's what it's for." *Who are you trying to fool?* Mia turned to her computer and ran her fingers across the keyboard. Within seconds multiple smaller windows appeared on her screen. An image in a center box immediately caught her attention. Mia exited out of the other windows, expanding the one that held her greatest interest. She stared at the muscular vision wearing black biker's shorts and tennis shoes and had sweat running down his broad, bare chest. He was pedaling on the NordicTrack machine.

"Oh, my..." Mia sat back and watched Keylan work out and his arm, thigh and chest muscles began to contract. Mia felt a warm tingling sensation building between her legs and the need to cross them was too great to resist. She tightened her thigh muscles as they met, releasing a slow, labored breath. She ran her right hand slowly across her lips, over her chin and down her neck as she closed her eyes. Mia began to wonder what it would be like to be the beneficiary of all the exertion as her hips began to sway in her seat.

"You all right, boss lady?"

Mia's eye's popped opened. She dropped her hands and sat up in the chair.

Sandra stood in the doorway, her mouth twisted upward. "I did knock."

"Excuse me…oh, yes, well… I guess I didn't hear you," she explained, hoping her face wasn't as red as Sandra's lipstick.

Sandra slowly walked up to Mia's desk. "I was coming to ask if you wanted to check out what we found on the security feed but it looks like you found it for yourself."

Mia felt horribly embarrassed at being caught gawking at Keylan. She dropped her head in her hands. "How long have you been standing there?" she murmured through her fingers.

"Long enough to see you sitting back squirming in your chair." Sandra laughed.

Mia dropped her hands and gave Sandra the evil eye.

"Don't look at me like that. I'm not the one who's in here gawking at a walking wet dream and getting all hot and bothered. Thank goodness the door was closed."

"I wasn't…" Sandra raised her left eyebrow. "Okay, maybe I was."

"You were what?" a baritone voice asked.

Sandra swung toward the sound and Mia quickly rose from her chair, tilting it backward. "Keylan…"

"Ladies," he replied, crossing his arms at his chest, which was now covered by a black muscle shirt. "Am I interrupting anything?"

"Not at all," Mia replied, hoping her face was less crimson than a few moments ago.

"Pardon my appearance—"

"It's fine," Sandra said, giving him a nonchalant wave and offering him a wide, wolflike smile.

"Actually it isn't," Mia said, glaring at her friend.

"Trust me, I know the rules. I needed to retrieve my bag from my car." He held up a black-leather Gucci carrier. "I was hoping I could convince you to have lunch with me so we can discuss some of the recommended changes I sent you to review. I'd love to hear your thoughts."

Mia brought her left hand to her hip, shifting her weight from one leg to the other. "Oh, now you want to have a discussion, after you've already implemented several things on your list."

Keylan shrugged and walked into the office. "While I'll always welcome everyone's input, I was left in charge. It's our family foundation, so funding any changes I want to make won't be a problem. Besides, the few improvements I've implemented were no-brainers. Having a professional chef brings order and structure to the kitchen. Updating the meal program to include something a little fresher and expanding the Meals on Wheels outreach to include both lunch and dinner is the right thing to do when there's such a need. Who could possibly object to any of those things?"

Mia dropped her hand and sighed. "You're right, and while I'd really like to discuss your ideas, we have a lunch meeting."

"Oh, yeah, about that." Sandra turned her attention to Mia. "That was the other thing I wanted to tell you when I came in here. I guess I got sidetracked." Sandra winked at Mia.

"Like now." Mia's eyes narrowed.

Sandra laughed. "The lunch got rescheduled." Her eyes darted back to Keylan. "Looks like she's free, after all."

"Great. I'll just go change and bring our food back and we can get to work."

"Fine."

After Keylan left the office, Sandra turned and faced Mia. "You can thank me later."

"Thank you for what?" Mia asked, glaring at her friend as if she didn't know who she was.

"Oh, give me a break. I realize you've taken this long vow of celibacy but you've clearly been affected by that man," she insisted.

Mia sat in her chair and turned to her computer. "Don't be ridiculous."

Sandra brought both hands to her hips. "Then what exactly were you doing when I walked in here a few minutes ago?"

Losing my mind. "Have you started working on the added verbiage for the new teaching positions we want to fill?"

"I was, but I guess you weren't the only one who got distracted," she said, laughing.

Mia ignored her comment. "Can you email me the final list of participants for this weekend's bowling tournament?"

"Sure thing, boss lady." Sandra walked out of the office.

Keylan showered, changed back into his suit and was preparing to head to the kitchen to collect lunch for himself and Mia when his phone rang. He smiled at the stunning face that popped up on his screen. "Good afternoon, China."

"Good afternoon to you, too. How's it going?"

"So far, so good. How's my favorite sister-in-law doing?"

A small giggle came through the phone. "I'm your only sister-in-law, KJ...kind of."

China Kingsley, an environmental lawyer and lead counsel for Kingsley Oil and Gas, was married to Keylan's eldest brother, Alexander.

"What's up?"

"I'm just checking to see if you have any questions about everything that's going on with the company. I know you got the message regarding our response to the media."

Keylan laughed. "You know I did. 'Kingsley Oil and Gas takes the safety of our employees very seriously and we're working closely with the US government to resolve these ridiculous charges.' Did I get that right?"

"Yes, you did. How are you and Mia getting along?"

"The jury is still out. Mia's beautiful, but she's tough," he informed her.

"That she is, and she's very good at her job," China assured him.

"I can see that. Why haven't we made her executive director of the foundation?"

"Aunt Elizabeth tried. Mia prefers being Elizabeth's second and the activities director. I think it's the time restraints that come with such a busy and visible role. She's a single mother, you know."

"Yes, I know. Colby is a great kid, cute and smart, too."

The phone went silent. "Hello... China, you still there?"

"Oh, I'm here. I'm just trying to wrap my head around the fact that you got a thing for a woman with a child."

"Who told you that? Travis?" He raised his voice slightly.

"He might've mentioned it, but I told him I'd have to hear you confirm it before I believed it, and you just did."

"Did not," he said, sounding like a little kid.

"Oh, but you did. Talking about Mia like that was a hint.

Adding your impressions about her son was the final tipping point," China concluded.

"I think since getting pregnant and marrying my brother you're seeing and hearing love and relationships everywhere," Keylan declared.

"If you say so. I heard about the suspension. Are you okay? You appealing it?"

"I don't know. I'm letting my attorney and agent deal with it. I'm just focusing on rehabbing my knee and now the foundation."

"And Mia…" she added, making kissing sounds.

"Really?"

"Keylan and Mia kissing in a tree…" China sang.

"On that note, I'll talk to you later." Keylan disconnected the phone and continued down the hall toward the kitchen, murmuring, "Me and Mia, right…"

Chapter 8

Mia laid all the files and contracts she believed they would be reviewing on her conference table. She returned to her desk and pulled her makeup bag from her purse. She powdered her face, freshened up her lipstick and made sure her hair was pinned up tightly in its bun. "What are you doing?" Mia closed her compact and returned it to her purse. "This is a business lunch."

"Ready for me?" Keylan said, walking into the office carrying a tray with two plates with silver cloches.

Mia rose from her seat. "Sure, come in." She gestured with her hand to the conference table. "Everything is completely organized for your review. I thought we could jump right into things while we eat."

Keylan placed the tray on the table. "Of course you did. I asked Donna to make us something special."

"What, no fish tacos?"

Keylan pulled out her chair, placed his hand at the small of her back and guided her to the seat. "Please sit."

His gentle touch and the sweet, musky scent emanating from his body assaulted her senses, sending Mia's body up in flames. She smiled at him and complied. "Thank you."

Keylan placed a covered plate in front of Mia and lifted the top. The plate held four palm-size tacos: two fish and two shrimp with two different sauces. Mia took a whiff. "This smells wonderful."

"Wait until you taste it. Shoot, I forgot the drinks."

"No worries. I have water and juice," she said, pointing to the small black refrigerator in the left corner of the room. She started to rise.

"I'll get it." Keylan walked over to the refrigerator and bent down. Mia couldn't help but admire how well his pants fit his butt.

Keylan opened the refrigerator door and laughed. "What's so funny?" she questioned before sticking her pinky finger in the green sauce and then placing it on her tongue.

"When you said you had water and juice, I didn't think you meant mini water bottles and juice pouches." Keylan picked up two pouches. "What's your pleasure, grape or fruit punch?" His mouth curved into a smile.

Mia smiled. "I'll take the fruit punch."

"Me, too." Keylan closed the door and returned to the table. "If you open my brothers' or even my mother's refrigerator, for that matter, you'll find beer, wine and soda. And the soda is for adding to the alcohol."

"I can imagine your aunt Elizabeth's refrigerator probably looks closer to mine than theirs."

"You're probably right. Here you go." He handed Mia a pouch.

"Thank you. I thought we could go over your recommended changes first," Mia said, reaching for her files.

"And I think we should eat first," he said, lifting the lid from his plate. "Donna makes the best seafood tacos." Keylan took the green sauce and poured it over his fish tacos. "Her avocado sauce is fantastic, too."

Mia followed Keylan's lead, adding sauce to her tacos before taking a bite. "Mmm…so good," she said with her eyes closed.

* * *

Damn. The sound and look of satisfaction on Mia's face sent a wave of desire through Keylan that had him grateful to be sitting down. "Donna really is an amazing chef," he agreed before taking a bite into his own tacos.

Mia picked up her drink, used the attached straw and poked it into the pouch. She wrapped her mouth around the straw and took a pull. It was a move that made Keylan reach under the table to adjust himself.

"I must admit, adding Donna to the staff and embracing a more organic and fresh menu is a pretty good idea. A surprising one, too."

"Surprising how?"

"I've had dinner with your family. They love their steak."

Keylan laughed. "Yes, we do. However, I also love my fruits and vegetables as long as they're fresh."

"It must be an athletic thing, having a balanced diet, I guess." Mia took another bite of her food.

Keylan nodded. "Can I ask you a personal question?"

"Depends." Mia took another drink from her pouch.

"On what exactly?"

Mia covered her mouth and said, "On how personal the question may be."

"Fair enough." Keylan got up and walked over to the refrigerator. He opened the door and pulled out two bottles of water and returned to the table. He handed one to Mia.

"What, you didn't like the fruit punch?" she asked, laughing.

"One's my limit. I'm driving."

Mia smiled. "So what's your question?"

Keylan wiped his mouth with a napkin and tossed it onto his empty plate. "Colby has few of the physical characteristics associated with Down syndrome and those that he has are less prominently visible. Does Colby have Mosaic Down syndrome?"

Mia's eyes went wide. "Yes. Colby has a percentage of cells with the extra chromosome number twenty-one associated with Down syndrome. How do you—?"

"How do I know about Mosaic Down? I just do."

Mia slid her plate forward. "There's definitely a story there."

Keylan folded his arms across his chest. "How about I tell you my story and you tell me yours?"

"Mine…?"

"Yes. Why don't you celebrate Christmas?"

"You first," she said, cracking the seal of her water bottle.

"We were all home-schooled when we were younger. When I was in eighth grade, we started having school here."

Mia's eyebrows came to attention. "At the foundation?"

"Yep. You know what happened to my father and uncle, right?" he asked, taking a drink from his water bottle.

"Yes, they died in a plane crash that they piloted, right?"

Keylan nodded as he held the bottle to his lips. He brought it down and said, "Their death sent my family into a tailspin for a really long time." Keylan broke eye contact for several seconds as he fought to keep his emotions under control. "We all found ways to distract ourselves from the pain of the loss, as well as all the unsettling changes that followed. I had a friend that had Down syndrome and I wanted to learn everything I could about the disease. I became obsessed with researching it. His symptoms were so light some people couldn't tell anything was different about him. He explained to me how the chromosome count worked and that he had Mosaic Down syndrome. Colby reminds me of my friend. His name is Raul."

"Where's Raul now?"

Keylan missed his friend and a wave of sadness came over him. "He and his family live in Florida. My schedule doesn't make it easy but we try to see each other a couple of times a year."

"That's nice. Colby's physical symptoms, appearance-wise—his facial features—are slight, as well. He has *some* respiratory issues but his intellectual disability is mild. He's like any other four-year-old boy, except he's usually very shy and timid around people he doesn't know," she explained.

"He's an amazing kid," he commented.

"I know," she said, smiling at the compliment.

Keylan could see the tears Mia was trying to hide as she stood and collected their trash, dumping it in the can next to her desk. "Your turn. What is it about Christmas that makes it like just another day for you?"

Mia used the hand sanitizer on her desk. She turned, faced Keylan and held up the bottle. "Care for some?"

Keylan smiled, rose from his seat and walked up to Mia. "I most certainly would."

Mia shook her head and said, "Is this you trying to be charming?" She squirted the gel in his hands.

Keylan stared down at Mia. He rubbed his hands together and the corners of his mouth lifted before he replied, "You are the most beautiful woman I have ever seen."

Mia's mouth mimicked his. "Thank you, but we really should keep things between us professional." She held his gaze before stepping around him, returning to her seat at the conference table.

Too much. "So Christmas…?"

Mia groaned. "I told Colby's biological father that I was pregnant Christmas Day, thinking it would be a wonderful way to celebrate all our holidays moving forward."

"I'm guessing it didn't go over well," Keylan observed.

"No, he denied he was the father and ended our relationship."

"Seriously?"

Her mouth set in a tight line. "Yep, even though he knew he'd been the only man I'd ever been with."

"I'm sorry."

Mia shrugged. "I guess having a wife and kid at his side as he entered the NBA draft wasn't part of his plans."

"Did he make it to the NBA?"

"For a while. Now he's playing somewhere overseas."

"He's not even a man. You shouldn't let the actions of one ass ruin Christmas for you."

"How about the actions of two asses?"

Keylan frowned. "What do you mean?"

"When I was a little girl, my mother decided she didn't want to be a mother anymore. Can you guess what day she had that great revelation?"

"You have got to be kidding me."

"Not at all," she said nonchalantly, reaching for her stacks of folders. "That's enough of walking down memory lane. How about we get down to business?"

Keylan felt a strong sense of anger and sadness for the stunning woman sitting across from him, trying her best to appear as though she hadn't been deeply affected by the betrayal of those she'd trusted the most. Keylan accepted the files she handed to him and asked, "Where would you like to start?"

They spent the next few hours going over all of Keylan's recommendations, including plans for the weekend's upcoming charity event, as well as the best way to handle the predicted media firestorm they were expecting with everything going on with their company and Keylan's suspension.

He found Mia's questions and concerns to be smart and

well thought out. She was not only gorgeous and sexy as hell; he thought she was intelligent and very compassionate. Keylan caught himself wondering what it would be like to kiss her. How it would feel to have those hands she talked with explore his body.

"So you think we should take ten to fifteen kids on a summer and winter vacation?"

"Excuse me?" Keylan said, embarrassed to have been caught not listening.

Mia repeated her question. And while she was in agreement with the majority of Keylan's outlined recommendations, the suggestion that they take kids on vacations was clearly giving her pause.

"Sure, why not? Look, most of these kids never have a chance to leave Houston, let alone the state, for such an amazing opportunity."

"I realize that and spending a weekend at your family's ranch would be a good idea. But taking kids on a ski trip is a bit much, don't you think?"

"Not at all. These kids need to be introduced to new adventures. I think you could use a little adventure yourself," he proclaimed. "In fact, we should take a quick trip so you can see for yourself what I have in mind."

"I'm not—"

"It's a business trip. You'll have your own space, and I'm always the perfect gentleman. Unless you ask me not to be." He gifted her with a sexy smile.

"Excuse me," Sandra said as she entered the office. "Mia, you have a conference call in ten minutes and, KJ, you told me to remind you when Coach Hooper was starting her playtime with the kids."

Keylan checked his watch. "Oh, wow, I can't believe it's after three." He stood and collected his notes from the meeting. "We'll continue this tomorrow."

* * *

Mia watched Keylan walk out the door, feeling like everything she'd thought she knew about the man might not be true, and she didn't know how she felt about that fact.

"Are you all right?" Sandra asked, frowning.

"What? Yes, of course." Mia shook her head and returned to her desk. "Why are you asking?"

"You look…confused." Sandra gave her a sideways look.

"Don't be ridiculous. Do I have all the reports I need for my call?"

Sandra placed her hands on her hips. "Yes. I emailed you all the reports you requested."

"Great." Mia reached for her desk phone. "Let's get back to work."

Unfortunately "tomorrow" seemed to be elusive to both Mia and Keylan. For the next few days they were like two ships passing each other at sea. Their interactions at the office were brief and professional. Just the way she wanted it…or so she thought. The media attention around Keylan and the Kingsleys' business was intense. They'd hired additional security to ensure everyone's safety and privacy was protected. Between Keylan's rehab schedule, his personal business responsibilities and acting as executive director for their foundation, he was busy.

Mia couldn't understand why Keylan's demanding schedule annoyed her so much, since he was meeting all his commitments at the foundation and with the kids. Especially Colby. She knew her annoyance toward Keylan was personal, yet she wasn't sure how she wanted to deal with her feelings. A physical attraction was one thing; an emotional pull was something else entirely.

Chapter 9

Mia stood at the registration table that had been set up just inside the doors of the bowling alley the Kingsleys had commandeered for their annual bowling tournament. The large twenty-four-lane facility had been redesigned and branded in such a way that left no doubt who was sponsoring the event. The Kingsley Foundation name and logo were everywhere. Mia had stuffed bags with candy and other goodies for the kids as she'd watched the final touches being put in place.

"Good morning," Sandra greeted her, handing Mia a cup of coffee.

"Thank you," she said, accepting the cup with a big smile. "And good morning to you, too."

"Wow, this place looks great and completely different from the last time I was here."

Mia nodded. "Yep, Victoria and Elizabeth basically gutted the place and put their own stamp on it."

"Did they buy the bowling alley?"

"Not outright. It's an investment," Mia explained.

"A bowling alley?"

Mia shrugged. "Rich people."

"Well, it looks great and I love how open it is now. You can see everything as soon as you walk in the place. All the wide lanes, state-of-the-art game rooms for the kids and adults and two large concession stands. But my favorite thing is the two massive bars in the middle of the place... one for kids and one for adults. What a great idea."

"I know," Mia replied before taking another sip of her coffee.

"I love these event shirts, too." Sandra looked down at the one she wore.

"Nothing says Kingsley Foundation more than a white T-shirt with their name surrounded by kids' handprints."

"Where's Colby?"

"He's with my aunt. He'll be here later," Mia explained.

"And KJ? I'm surprised he's not here yet." Sandra looked around the room.

Mia placed her cup on the table and went back to stuffing her bags. "I have no idea. It's eight o'clock on a Saturday morning. There's no telling what or who he was into last night, but I'm sure he'll stroll in here at some point before everything gets started."

Sandra gave Mia the evil eye. "What's up with you? That was even catty for me."

Mia picked up her coffee and took another drink. "I don't know what you're talking about." *Yeah, you do, and she's right.*

Sandra started stuffing bags with candy. "KJ's been great these past few days. What makes you think he'll slack off now?"

Mia offered a dismissive wave. "Never mind me, I'm just tired and anxious about the event."

"Why? Everything looks great and we've got nearly all the lanes sold. It still amazes me how people line up to give ten thousand just to bowl with a bunch of old people."

"Really? Many bowling champions and athletes are donating their time to our cause."

"I guess, but it's still bowling. I could see golf. It was cool how KJ got some of his teammates to participate. Thank goodness, they didn't have a game."

"Yeah, and next week's game is in town."

A wide smile spread across Sandra's face. "Someone's been checking out the schedule."

"Have not... Well, maybe I glanced at it."

Sandra nudged Mia with her elbow. "Go for it, girl. He's obviously interested in you and I know you like him."

"Oh, please." Mia turned away from Sandra and started opening another box of bags. "Even if I did like him like that, and I'm not saying that I do, men like him have limited interest when it comes to women."

"You might have a point."

Mia could hear the change in Sandra's voice. She turned to ask why when she saw for herself.

Keylan, who was wearing jeans, their event T-shirt and his branded sneakers, was walking through the door with a beautiful, tall, athletically built woman at his side. They were laughing as they made their way to the table.

"Good morning, ladies." Keylan greeted the women with a smile.

"Good morning, KJ," Sandra replied.

She's far too beautiful to be anything other than a runway model and his girlfriend. No wonder he's been so busy.

Who cares... Stop it and focus.

"Morning," Mia said, her tone flat.

"This is my friend Becky B. She plays guard for the Rivers."

See, she's just his friend. Wait, why are you so invested in this man's personal life? Stop it!

"And the baddest sister in the WNBA." Sandra complimented, extending her hand.

Becky B shook her hand, saying, "Thanks, but I think Cynthia Cooper would disagree with you."

Sandra nodded. "She's cool, too."

"It's nice meeting you," Mia said, shaking her hand.

"Where do you want me?" she asked.

"How about lane twelve? I want you right in the center of all the action." Keylan pointed in the direction of the lanes.

"Sounds good to me," Becky replied, rubbing her hands together.

"Sandra, can you please hook Becky B up with one of our event shirts?" Keylan asked.

"Sure thing, follow me, Becky." Sandra waved her forward.

"So…" Mia went back to stuffing bags.

"So…what?" Keylan leaned against the table.

"You invited Becky B as your special guest or something?" She kept her eyes on her bags.

"Actually, I invited Becky B and a few more of my friends to come help out today. You know, raise the bar a bit." Keylan picked up one of the bags and started examining its contents.

Mia brought both hands to her hips. "Excuse me. Raise the bar?"

"Yeah, I mean this little event has been fine—"

"Fine! I'll have you know that we raise nearly fifty thousand dollars a year for local charities, which the foundation matches, putting on this *little* event." She emphasized the word, frowning.

"Don't take my comments personally." Keylan placed the bag on the table. "I've told my aunt for years that she needed to bump up the glam factor in order to raise more money."

"'Bump up the glam factor,'" she repeated, folding her

arms across her chest, shifting her weight from her left to her right leg.

"Yes. See, what I have in mind is adding a special guest to play with each team and expanding from twelve teams to twenty-four. Our new theme is bowling with special guests," he explained excitedly.

"So you're just going to change the game plan…today?" she asked, not even trying to hide her anger.

"It's just a change to how the teams will be structured. That's all."

"And what about the kids? Half of the lanes have been earmarked for them, so they can participate, too. Your plan is to just, what? Keep them in the game room and out of the way during the whole event?" Her face went blank and her voice had taken on a harsh tone.

"Whoa, calm down." He held up both hands. "That's not at all what I had in mind. The kids *are* the special guests. Each team of four will consist of one celebrity type and one of our kids. The forty-eight folks we have signed up will be divided among the twenty-four teams. I spent the last couple of days recruiting people to not only make a donation, doubling the financial gains to our cause, but to give up a couple of hours of their time, too. I didn't want to say anything until I knew I could pull it off. I wouldn't want to disappoint you."

Way to go, Mia. You jumped to conclusions about him again. Mia dropped her arms and lowered her eyes briefly before meeting his gaze again. "That's actually a wonderful idea," she conceded.

"Did that hurt much?" Keylan asked, the corners of his mouth turning up.

Mia returned to stuffing her bags. "Little bit."

Keylan threw his head back and released a laugh that

captured several bystanders' attention. "Gotta love your honesty."

Keylan's smile and laughter sent waves of desire through Mia's body. She needed a distraction so she checked her watch and asked, "So where're the rest of your recruits?"

Before he could respond he heard, "KJ, you ready to get schooled, son?"

Mia turned toward the sound. Her mouth opened and quickly closed as she watched several sports stars from football, basketball, baseball and even hockey walk through the door.

"How?" she asked, her eyes wide.

Keylan leaned down and whispered, "I have a lot of friends and I'm very good at convincing people to do what I want."

The warmth of Keylan's breath on her skin and the masculine smell of his cologne had her light-headed. "I bet," she murmured.

Keylan returned to his full height. "Excuse me while I go direct everyone to where they need to go."

Mia watched as Keylan shook hands with his friends before leading them to the table where they collected their event shirts. "That man is nothing like you expected," she murmured.

After leading each celebrity to their assigned lanes, Keylan stood and watched Mia as she coordinated everyone's activities and movements from the bar placed in the middle of the room. She was like a conductor directing her orchestra. He laughed at how fast her short legs moved her from one spot to the other. His body stirred when she bent to pick up something she'd dropped. He had to stop his mind and body from reacting to sexy thoughts while he stood in the middle of such a public place.

"I'm here, cuz. Where do you want me?" Travis asked, walking up behind Keylan.

Keylan turned and greeted his cousin with a fist bump. "You'll be playing on lane seventeen."

"Cool." Travis took in his surroundings. "Wow, this place looks great. I love the adult bar and the old-fashioned soda and ice cream station for the kids. There's a little something for everyone."

"Yeah, Aunt Liz's idea. You have to check out the game rooms. There's one for kids and adults. The adult one has everything you'd want in a man cave."

Travis smirked. "That's my mother for you. So, where's your girl?"

"My girl?" Keylan replied, knowing exactly who he was referring to.

"Yes, Mia. I don't see her." Travis turned and scanned the room again.

"She's not my girl and she's in the lounge," Keylan confirmed.

"Keeping up with her?" Travis teased.

Yes. "No."

"Why don't you just ask her out already?" Travis leaned against the bar.

"Look, we talked about—"

"Excuse me, Mr. Kingsley." A young woman wearing a foundation volunteer shirt interrupted the two men. "They need you in the lounge. Miss Mia hurt herself."

Keylan took off running toward the lounge with Travis on his heels. His heart was beating so fast he just knew Travis could hear it pounding.

Keylan walked into the lounge to find Mia standing in front of a small sink with her left hand under the faucet. There was blood-stained gauze littering the counter and the floors.

"Hold still, Mia," Sandra demanded.

"It's fine. I just need to wrap it up," Mia insisted.

"We've tried that…twice. You need a doctor." Sandra's nose crinkled.

"What happened?" Keylan asked as he walked up and stood behind Mia.

"It's nothing," Mia replied.

"It doesn't look like nothing to me." Keylan's jaw clenched.

"She cut her hand with a box cutter," Sandra volunteered as she wrapped Mia's hand in a towel. "We can't seem to stop the bleeding for very long."

"You need to get to a doctor," Travis suggested.

"No, I just need a few butterfly stitches. We sent some-one for the large first-aid kit in the office," Mia explained matter-of-factly.

"That's about a three-inch cut—you need some sutures," Keylan countered. "Excuse me, Sandra. May I?" He held out his left hand and Sandra released Mia's into his. He gently held Mia's hand while he unwrapped the towel. Her skin was soft and delicate, and Keylan suddenly had the urge to kiss it, as if that could make it better. "Yep, you need sutures."

"Here's the kit," another volunteer said, walking into the lounge.

"That won't be necessary." Keylan pulled out his keys and stared down at Mia. "I'm taking you to urgent care."

Chapter 10

Mia still couldn't believe how insistent Keylan had been in getting her to a doctor. He made her feel a certain kind of way: protected and cared for, when she knew she shouldn't allow such feelings to creep into her heart. "This is ridiculous," Mia complained, sitting in an exam room of the nearby urgent care facility. "The bleeding has slowed down considerably."

"Yes, but it hasn't stopped," Keylan said, keeping his eye on the magazine he was reading as he sat across from the exam table where Mia was perched.

"Sandra could have driven me, you know."

"I know." Keylan flipped another page.

The exam room door opened. "Good morning, Ms. Ramirez. I'm Dr. Moon." The handsome doctor introduced himself as he entered the room, reading her name from a tablet. "I understand you have a nasty cut."

"That she does," Keylan offered.

"Oh, wow, KJ. Nice to meet you, man," Dr. Moon replied, his eyes wide with surprise as he extended his hand.

"Nice to meet you, too. Her hand is a mess." Keylan stood and shook the doctor's hand.

"Let's let the doctor make that determination, if you don't mind," Mia said, giving Keylan the evil eye.

The doctor washed and dried his hands before putting on a pair of latex gloves. He removed the towel and examined Mia's hand. "That's a pretty deep cut. May I ask how this happened?"

"I was careless with a box opener," Mia explained.

"If you would've asked, I would have taken care of it for you," Keylan chastised, moving to stand next to Mia.

"I'm perfectly capable of handling things myself." *Yeah, if you hadn't been thinking about him.*

"Really now?" He offered her a lazy smile.

The doctor cleared his throat. "You're going to need a few stitches. I'll clean and medicate your wound, stitch you up, and you'll need a tetanus shot, too."

"Um…a tetanus shot?" Mia bit her bottom lip.

"Wait—don't tell me Miss I Can Handle Things Myself is afraid of a little shot," Keylan teased.

Mia glared up at Keylan as the doctor pulled out a surgical tray and started working on her hand.

"This may sting a bit. It's a liquid antibiotic."

"Would you like me to hold your other hand?" Keylan smirked.

Mia rolled her eyes. "Go ahead, Doctor. I'll be fine."

Keylan's phone rang and he read the screen. "Excuse me for a moment." He got up and left the room.

Mia was relieved that Keylan stepped out. She couldn't figure out what was making her more light-headed: Keylan's nearness or the open cut the doctor was working on.

She watched as the doctor clipped the last stitch. "That wasn't too bad, now, was it?" he asked as he started wrapping her hand. "You'll have to keep these stitches clean and dry."

"No problem," she promised, examining her hand.

The doctor reached for the syringe that had been lying on the tray, mocking Mia, and she turned her head. She would never admit it to Keylan but she hated needles. "This won't hurt—"

"Good, I didn't miss the shot," Keylan said, walking back into the exam room.

"Don't mind him, Doctor. I'm ready." Mia closed her eyes.

"We're done," the doctor said soon after, dropping the needle cartridge and the syringe filled with saline in a red biohazard box.

"What, you're done? I didn't feel a thing." Mia's eyes were wide with surprise.

"I know. You were so focused on the syringe you didn't notice the needle pin right next to it. It's new. There is a numbing substance supplied at the same time the injection is given. The syringe was just a distraction."

"Wow, talk about a great invention. I know a little boy who would really appreciate something like that," she said, laughing.

"Where is the little man, anyway?" Keylan asked, looking down at Mia's hand.

"With my aunt, but he'll be at the bowling alley later this afternoon."

The doctor removed his gloves and said, "I'm going to need to see you back here in about a week. You'll need to change that dressing daily."

"She will, I'll make sure of it," Keylan promised.

"You'll make sure of it?" Mia replied, bumping her hand against the table, wincing.

Keylan cupped her face with his left hand. "Are you okay?"

Mia could see the worry in his eyes and her heart flipped. It was a look similar to that Colby often gave her when he, too, was worried that something might be wrong. "I... I'm fine."

Keylan dropped his hand. "You have got to be careful."

"You can take ibuprofen for the pain," Dr. Moon advised, "but if that doesn't help, I can call you in something a little stronger."

"Thanks but that won't be necessary," she said.

The doctor pulled out a business card and handed it to Keylan. "If she changes her mind, just give me a call."

"Thanks, Doc." Keylan put the card in his back pants' pocket. "Do you have a back exit?"

"Yes, of course. It's across from the fire exit. I'll go get the code. I'll be right back."

"A back exit? Why?" Mia frowned up at Keylan.

"It appears somehow the press figured out we were here."

"How? I mean, we were careful when we left the bowling alley. We even took Travis's car."

"We were careful when we left. Not so much while we waited in the lobby."

"Oh, no." Mia lowered her head and covered her eyes with her right hand. "I guess I'll be splattered all over the paper tomorrow."

Keylan's face went blank. "Tomorrow?" He pulled out his phone and did an online search for his name before he handed Mia the phone. "We've already hit the internet. I bet we'll be trending by the time we get back to the bowling alley."

Mia read the headline: KJ and Mystery Woman at Local Clinic. Why?

"Great, just great. At least they don't have my name."

"Not yet, but it's only a matter of time." Keylan's expression dulled.

Mia scowled. "Aren't you just the bearer of good news?"

The door opened and the doctor poked his head in. "All

clear and I've deactivated the fire alarm. Take all the time you need."

"Thanks, Doc." Keylan shook his hand.

"Yes, thank you, Doctor, for everything," Mia added.

Keylan stood in front of Mia with his hands in his pockets, smiling down at her. "You ready to blow this Popsicle stand?"

"I guess so."

Keylan placed his hands on both sides of Mia's waist and lifted her off the exam table and onto the floor. Her heart was pounding so fast she just knew it would burst through her chest. "Th-thank you," Mia whispered.

"You're welcome." Keylan pushed a wayward strand of hair behind her ear. He slowly slid his hand down the side of Mia's face before dropping it and taking a step back. "Shall we?"

After a short ride Keylan and Mia were back at the bowling alley, where they found all the events and activities were under way. Keylan leaned against the ice cream bar and watched all the action from his vantage point when he heard "Keylan!"

Keylan turned to find Colby, dressed in blue jeans, an event T-shirt and those Velcro shoes he hated, running toward him with an older couple following close behind, both dressed in the adult version of Colby's outfit.

"Keylan," Colby called again, wrapping his arms around Keylan's legs.

"Hey, little man," Keylan said, squatting to meet Colby's eye level. "How are you?"

"I'm fine."

"Good afternoon, Mr. Kingsley. I'm Colby's great-aunt Mavis and this is my husband, Rudy," the woman announced.

Keylan rose, keeping a tight hold to Colby's hand. "Pleased to meet you both," he said, shaking both of their hands. "Please call me Keylan."

"Have you seen my niece?" Mavis asked.

"Can I see Mommy?" he asked, his eyes wide.

Keylan smiled down at Colby. "Yes, Colby, you can see your mommy."

Keylan returned his attention to the curious faces of the couple before him.

"I understand you and my niece are working together at the foundation these days," Mavis continued.

"Yes, ma'am, and it's been a privilege." A wide smile crawled across his face.

"When do you think you'll be returning to the Carriers? They can use your help," Rudy asked.

Mavis nudged her husband with her elbow. "Excuse his insensitivity, my dear. How is your rehabilitation going?"

"It's going great, thank you for asking."

"Mommy…" Colby pulled his hand from Keylan's and ran to her. The small trio followed behind him.

Mia placed the tablet she'd been holding under her left arm and bent, held out her right arm and engulfed her son in a big hug and several kisses. "Hi, Colby, baby."

"I'm…no…baby," he declared between giggles. Mia looked up to see three sets of eyes staring down at her.

Mia stood, holding on to Colby's hand. "Aunt Mavis, Uncle Rudy, when did you get here?"

"Just now." Mavis leaned in and kissed her cheek. "Oh, my, what happened to your hand?"

"Mommy got a boo-boo?" Colby's face contorted.

Mia looked down at him. "Mommy's okay, baby." She returned her focus to her aunt and uncle. "I had a fight with a box cutter and lost."

"Has a doctor checked it out?" her uncle asked.

"Yes, sir. I took her to the urgent care down the street," Keylan explained.

"Did you, now?" Mavis replied, her eyes cutting to Mia.

"It was no trouble."

"Well, thank you for being so kind to my beautiful niece," Mavis said, smiling.

She most certainly is. "It was my pleasure," Keylan agreed; his eyes collided with Mia's.

"I wanna go play," he demanded, trying to pull his hand free from his mother as he used his free hand to point to the game room.

"Why don't you let me take Colby to the game room for a while?" Keylan offered.

Mia stared up at Keylan. "Really? You sure you don't mind?"

"I wouldn't have offered if I did," he assured her. "Colby is my main man."

"I'll join you," her uncle offered.

Mia squatted and said, "Colby, you stay with Keylan and Uncle Rudy. I'll see you in a few minutes."

"Okay." Colby pulled at Keylan's arm.

"Don't worry, he'll be fine. We'll see you in a bit, sweetheart," Uncle Rudy said.

"Yeah, what he said." Keylan let Colby pull him toward the game room.

"So, how's the hand?" Mavis asked, taking a seat at the soda bar, directing Mia to take the one next to her.

"It's fine. I was just a little careless."

Her aunt looked over her shoulder into the game room. "I can see *why* you may have been distracted."

"Not this again." Mia dropped her eyes to her tablet. It was one thing to try to hide her growing attraction from those who didn't know her well, but her aunt was a different story, especially when she was sitting right across from her.

"Yes, this again." Her aunt removed the tablet from Mia's hand and placed it on the bar. "We can either do this here, where I can pretend to accept a nice, watered-down version of the story while my heart breaks at the idea of my niece lying to me. Or we can go someplace where I can get a nice cup of coffee and settle in for the long, truthful version."

"Really, Auntie?" Mia gave her a lopsided grin. "You're laying it on pretty thick."

"Either way, you will fill me in on what's happening between you and that handsome hunk over there," she said, pointing at Keylan, who was carrying Colby on his shoulders. "Your choice."

"Some choice," she murmured, especially since she had no idea what was really going on between them.

Chapter 11

Mia slid off the stool. "Excuse me for a moment." She walked over to where Sandra had been standing doing her best impression of someone who wasn't eavesdropping. "Sandra, can you cover for me for a bit? I'm going to take my aunt to the office in the back."

Sandra smiled. "Need a little privacy to explain why you're trending on social media?"

"What?" Mia's eyebrows snapped together.

Sandra turned the tablet she held toward Mia. "See."

Mia ran her fingers up the screen, glancing through page after page all leading with basically the same topic: her. Who is Mia Ramirez? Is Mia Ramirez Keylan's New Lady? Why Were Mia and Keylan at the Clinic? "Oh, no. I knew about the story, but how did they get my name?"

"It's the media—they can do anything."

"Looks like my conversation with my aunt will take a little longer than I initially thought."

Sandra nodded. "I bet. Don't worry, I got you. And I'll keep an eye on Keylan for you, too," she said, wiggling her eyebrows.

"I'm sure you meant Colby."

"Yes, of course," she said, laughing.

Mia shook her head. "Thanks." Mia walked back over

to her aunt. "Let's go find someplace a little more private to talk."

"Good idea." Mavis picked up the two chocolate shakes she'd ordered and handed one to Mia. "For you. This is much better than coffee." She smiled before taking a pull from her straw.

"Follow me," Mia instructed.

"So you and my niece, what's the deal?" Rudy asked Keylan as both men stood back and watched Colby play with his friends.

"The deal?" Keylan echoed, knowing exactly what Mia's uncle was asking but not really sure he had an answer. It wasn't like he could say he thought she was the most beautiful and sexy woman he'd ever met and every time he got near her all he wanted to do was kiss her until they both couldn't breathe. He needed a real answer.

"Yes, son, the deal," Rudy repeated, glaring at Keylan.

"We're coworkers and friends. I think… I hope."

"Um, friends…*you think.*" Rudy's eyes bore into him. "Seems to me, son, there's a lot more than friendship going on between you two. I saw the way your face lit up like a lightbulb when she was hugging Colby."

"I think she's a great mom," he said, hoping Rudy was buying his explanation.

"That she is…and a beautiful woman."

And smart, strong and sexy as hell. Stop it. Keylan nodded, keeping his mouth shut, ensuring nothing crazy came tumbling out.

"She's also been through a lot and I don't want her hurt… Colby, either."

"I understand, sir."

Rudy shook his head. "I'm not sure you do. My wife thinks just because I have trouble hearing I don't know what's going on." He took a seat in a nearby chair. "What she doesn't realize is I hear and see everything that's important. Mia and Colby are very important. Now, sit down."

Keylan sat in the chair next to Rudy, both with a clear view of Colby who was jumping in a circle with his friends. "I'm seventy-five years old and I've experienced a lot in my life, so trust me when I say if you like—and I mean really like—someone, you had better tell them before someone else steps in and you lose your chance."

"What if I'm not sure if I'm good enough for someone like Mia?"

Rudy nodded slowly. "Women have no idea how uncomplicated and maybe even a little insecure we are when it comes to them."

"No, sir." Keylan leaned forward, resting his forearms on his knees. "No, sir, they certainly do not."

"I can't speak for Mia, so if you want to know if you are, there's only one way you're going to find out," he said, slapping Keylan on the back. "Now go get that boy so we can check out that ice cream bar before my wife comes back and reminds me why I shouldn't have it."

Both men laughed as Keylan went to collect Colby.

"Let me make sure I understand." Mavis sat back on the leather sofa in the office above the bowling alley. "You cut your hand, Keylan took you to the doctor and now you're all over the internet. Is that right?"

"Yes," Mia confirmed, biting her bottom lip. She felt like she was back in high school, explaining to her aunt why she'd decided to skip class with her friends to go to the beach after Mavis had specifically told her she couldn't go.

Mavis used her straw to stir her shake. "And why are you concerned about being all over the internet?"

"Because we're private people and folks are assuming Keylan and I are a couple," she explained.

"Why is that a bad thing?" Mavis took a drink of her shake.

"We discussed this already, Auntie. Keylan and I aren't dating."

"Well, maybe you should be," Mavis said before taking another sip from her cup.

"Auntie—"

"Okay, I'll drop it," she said, waving her right hand. "The least you can do is ask him over for dinner."

"And why is that the least I can do?"

The door opened and Sandra walked in before Mavis could respond to her niece. "Excuse me, Mia, but I thought you'd like to know that the games are winding down."

"Thanks, Sandra. How's Colby?"

"He's fine—they're having banana splits at the ice cream bar," Sandra informed both women.

"They?"

"Yes, your uncle and Keylan." Sandra walked out of the room, closing the door behind her.

"Now why should I invite Keylan to dinner?"

"He did take you to the doctor and made sure your hand was all right, didn't he?"

"Yes, but—"

"But nothing. It's the polite thing to do."

"He'll probably have other plans, anyway."

Mavis rose, dropped her empty cup into the trash can near the sofa and said, "There's only one way to find out, now, isn't there?" She opened the door and walked out of the room.

"Auntie..." Mia called, following after her.

"There you two are," Rudy cried out as his wife and niece approached.

"Just in time, too," Mavis said, coming to stand next to her husband. "If I know you—and I do, sir—you were about to order something else you shouldn't."

"Hi, Mommy," Colby yelled, keeping his seat next to Keylan.

"Hi, little man. Did you enjoy your ice cream?" Mia picked up a napkin and wiped Colby's face.

Colby nodded. "More, Mommy…"

"No, mister, and by the looks of that bowl, you've had plenty." Mia waited for a protest that didn't come.

Mia watched the glances and smiles shared between Keylan and Colby. There was a look of pride on both their faces, Keylan from the lessons he'd taught and Colby from learning them. "Um, thanks for looking after him for me," Mia said to Keylan.

"Anytime," he replied. Keylan's phone rang and he checked the screen. "Excuse me for a brief moment."

Mia watched as he walked away before bringing the phone to his ear.

"He seems all right." Rudy offered his unsolicited opinion.

Mia smiled at her uncle. "Think so?"

"I do, and Colby likes him, too, which is good enough for me," Rudy added.

"I told her to invite him over for dinner but your stubborn niece won't listen to me."

"I think that's a fine idea, Mia. You should do it," Rudy advised encouragingly.

"What's a fine idea?" Keylan asked, coming to stand behind Mia.

Mia could feel the warmth radiating off Keylan's body and his closeness was interrupting her ability to think. She wanted to move away from him but it was as if her feet were bolted to the floor. Between the heat from his body and the scent of his cologne, she was overwhelmed by Keylan's presence. "Answer the man, Mia," her aunt ordered.

Mia knew if she wanted to speak coherently she had to step away from Keylan, so she walked over and stood next to her uncle. "How would you like to have dinner tonight with me and Colby? It's my way of saying thanks for everything you did this morning." Mia held up her bandaged hand.

Mavis cleared her throat. "And…"

Mia looked at her aunt and frowned before looking back at Keylan. "And for keeping an eye on Colby for me."

"Both Colby and Rudy," Mavis added, smiling.

Keylan laughed. "It was completely my pleasure and I'd love to have dinner with you and Colby."

"Great, how's six?" Mia asked.

"Six it is. Text me your address."

"Sure." Mia scanned all the bowling lanes. "Looks like everyone's wrapping up. We should go make the presentation."

"You're right, we better go. I see that my aunt Elizabeth has arrived."

"Go on. We've got Colby." Mavis smiled at the little boy, who had made his way over to Keylan's side and was now holding his hand. Keylan looked down at Colby. "He can come with us. You don't mind, do you, Mia?"

"'Course not." Mia hugged her uncle and aunt. "We'll see you later."

"Shall we?" Keylan placed the palm of his free hand on the small of Mia's back. The warmth of his touch sent a wave of desire through Mia's body, making her stumble as she took a step.

"You all right?" Keylan asked, obviously holding back his laughter.

Not even a little bit— and you know it, too. "Sure, let's go," she replied, knowing that was the furthest thing from the truth.

Chapter 12

Keylan was standing in the middle of the living room of his penthouse suite in one of Houston's most exclusive downtown apartment buildings. He was trying to remember where he'd put his keys when his doorbell rang. He checked his watch and said, "Whoever that is can't stay. I won't be late for my date with Mia." He walked over to the door and opened it to the one person who moved at her own time and pace.

"Hello, darling," Victoria greeted him, stepping into his apartment without waiting for an invite, a tall, distinguished-looking gentleman following behind her.

"Hello, Mother, Mr. Rivers. What are you two doing here?" Keylan knew the way he asked the question might have sounded rude but all he wanted to do was get to Mia.

Victoria fell silent and offered her cheek for their usual greeting. Keylan smiled, leaned forward and kissed her. "Now, to answer your somewhat ridiculous question, Mr. Rivers is here to take photos and check the window and banister measurements for the lights and garland so he can get his team in here tomorrow to start decorating your apartment for the holidays. We're only a few weeks away from Christmas, you know."

"Yes, of course." Keylan walked around his sunken living room, hoping that height advantage would help in his search for his keys.

Victoria frowned at her son's actions as Rivers excused himself and started taking photos and notes. "What on earth are you doing, son?"

"I'm looking for my keys. I'm going to see Mia for six and I don't want to be late." Keylan had no idea why he'd blurted that out.

"A date?" she offered, sounding hopeful.

"No, it's just dinner," he snapped.

"Excuse me." Her voice was stern and tone deadpan. Victoria was a woman that didn't tolerate any form of disrespect, especially from her children.

Keylan and his mother had always had a complicated relationship. They were never as close as she had been with his brothers growing up. His father had died when he was very young and Victoria's priority had become keeping her family safe and growing their business, which had taken up a great deal of her time. Keylan might not have liked or even understood a number of things his mother did, but he loved her and respected her accomplishments.

Keylan stopped in his tracks. "I'm sorry, Mother. I'm just in a hurry and I can't find my keys."

Victoria glanced around the room. "You mean those keys?" She pointed to the bar in the corner of the room next to the door. "The ones sitting next to those very nice holiday gift bags."

Keylan's shoulders dropped and he released an audible sigh. "Yes, thank you."

"You seem awfully flustered for a man who's *only* having dinner," she said, giving him a knowing look.

"I'm not—I just don't want to be late. Mia already has this false narrative of me and I don't want to give her any reason to think she's right."

"Does she, now?" Victoria walked down the three steps and took a seat on his couch. "Come, tell me what she thinks she knows about you."

"I told you—"

"Sit down, Keylan," she ordered. "For heaven's sake, it's four thirty. The last time I checked, Mia only lived twenty minutes from here. You'll be there before five."

"Aren't you the one who's always drilled into us that being on time is really late?" he reminded, walking down the steps and joining his mother on the couch.

"Yes, and that's right when it comes to most things. However, leaving now puts you at Mia's an hour early. Trust me when I say single mothers need all the time they can get when preparing for a date."

"It's not…"

Victoria narrowed her eyes and held up her left hand. Keylan closed his mouth. He still couldn't believe how well such a simple gesture still worked on him and his brothers. "You have time for a nice chat with your mother."

"How would you know if it's difficult dating as a single mother? You never dated when we were kids and you had more help than any of us wanted around." Keylan's tone had more of an edge to it than he realized.

Victoria sat back and crossed her legs. She tilted her head slightly to the left and her expression closed up. "You've always been my most willful and outspoken child. I know everyone thinks that best describes your brothers Alexander and Morgan, and while they, too, love to challenge me, they never doubted my motive was my love for them."

"Mother, I—"

"When you were eight, you had a game you wanted me to attend but I had to go out of town on business. When I came to your room to say goodbye, you refused to look at me and you said that I didn't love you and you didn't care."

Keylan nodded. "I remember that. I was just a kid. I especially remember the beating Alexander and Morgan gave me for disrespecting you." He reached for his mother's hand and squeezed it. "I knew then, as I know now, just how much you love me, Mother."

Victoria released a loud breath. "I appreciate you saying that, son, but it really doesn't matter. It may not be the politically correct thing to say, and I realize my actions often left you angry and confused, but please understand that my love for all you children, Elizabeth and our business is what allowed me to put one foot in front of the other after your father died. You all gave me the strength I needed in order to make tough decisions that protected our family and grew our business. I won't apologize for that…ever."

"I understand."

"Mia…"

Keylan shrugged.

Victoria gave her son's hand a small shake and released it. "Now, tell me about today's event. According to Elizabeth, it went fabulously well."

"Colby, are you dressed?" Mia yelled out as she put the finishing touches to her salad.

"Yes, Mommy," he responded and ran into the kitchen wearing blue jeans and a light blue T-shirt, his feet bare.

"Colby, where are your socks?" Mia placed the salad in the refrigerator before turning to face her son.

"In the sock drawer, Mommy," he said, frowning up at her.

Mia couldn't help but laugh at the confused look on her son's face. "Okay, young man, why don't you go find a pair and put them on your feet?"

"Okeydoke." Colby ran out of the room.

It had been years since Mia had made dinner for any

man other than her uncle and she couldn't believe how nervous she was. "Get a grip, it's just a meal. He probably only said yes to be nice." Mia moved to her stove and turned off the burner under her simmering meat. "Let's see—my meat's ready, the salad's done and the buns are ready for the toaster." She checked her watch. "Time to get dressed."

Mia made her way to her bedroom, where she discarded the robe she had been wearing and slipped on a blue silk, scoop-necked dress. She pulled her curly hair up and clipped it high on her head before lightly dusting her face with makeup and applying a sheer lip gloss. Standing in front of her full-length mirror, she admired her dress from all angles before slipping her feet into a pair of black slipper sandals. "Well, this will have to do."

Mia checked the time and took a deep breath, releasing it slowly. She turned to find Colby standing in her doorway. "Keylan's coming… Keylan's coming," he announced, his face lit up like high beams on a car.

Well, let's go get this over with. "Let's go see."

"Yay…" Colby yelled, running to the door. He jumped on the bay window seat, looked out the window and announced, "He's…here."

Keylan pulled his black Mercedes into the driveway of the small, gray-brick house in the middle of a cul-de-sac. He exited the vehicle and laughed at the fact that Mia's house was the only one not decorated for Christmas. He walked up to the door and knocked, smiling and waving back at the excited, little curly-haired boy in the window whose smile brightened most of his days.

He stood at the door holding two gift bags he hoped would be received with the spirit in which they were intended. His heart raced at the sound of the door's lock being released and he murmured, "Man, chill."

The door opened and the striking woman that he couldn't seem to get off his mind stood before him, holding the hand of the cutest boy ever. Clearly, Mia was trying to stop him from bolting out the door.

"Good evening," Mia said, giving her son's hand a small shake.

"Hi, Keylan. You look like me." Colby gave Keylan a big, toothy grin.

"Hi, buddy, and you're right, except I have on a jacket and sneakers," Keylan replied before turning his attention to Mia. "Hello, Mia, you look breathtakingly beautiful." *Smooth, real smooth.*

Mia smiled. "Thank you. Please come in," she offered, stepping aside.

Keylan crossed the threshold into the small bungalow and smiled. The house was open and free of the clutter he'd expected in a house with a four-year-old boy. The furnishings were perfect in their simplicity and screamed "home sweet home." "You have a lovely place, Mia." *Not a sign of Christmas in sight in here, either. I must fix that.*

"Thanks, we like it."

"This is for Colby." He held up a medium-size gift bag. "I hope you don't mind."

Mia shook her head. "Not at all. Well, as long as it isn't something sweet."

"Well, I think it's pretty sweet but if you're worried it's something to eat, don't be. May I?" he asked, looking down at Colby.

"Of course."

Keylan stooped to Colby's eye level. "Here you go, man. Why don't you check this out?" He handed Colby the bag. Keylan rose, turned back and faced Mia. "This is for you."

Mia accepted the smaller gift bag and pulled out a bottle of Mer Soleil Chardonnay. A wide smile spread across her face. She didn't have any real vices but she did enjoy a nice bottle of wine. "One of my favorites, how did you know?" Mia held the bottle to her chest.

"A little bird told me," he confessed.

"Well, thank you and your little bird," she said, holding his gaze.

"You are more than welcome." Keylan felt his body start to stir and a magnetic pull had him leaning forward. He figured a quick kiss couldn't hurt when he heard, "Look, Mommy. I'm just like Keylan."

Chapter 13

Mia's body was responding to Keylan's presence in a way that she was beginning to get used to and even enjoy. She often found herself daydreaming about how it would feel to be kissed and touched by a man she wasn't sure would be good for her or her son. Gazing up into Keylan's light brown eyes drew her to him like a giant magnet, and that was both exciting and very scary.

Mia took a step toward Keylan when she heard, "Mommy..." She quickly turned to face her son. "Yes, darling."

"I'm just like Keylan." He held up a pair of black sneakers with Keylan's signature on the sides of each shoe in white script.

"Wow, those are...great." Mia's eyes danced between her son and Keylan. *What was he thinking?* "What do you say?"

"Thank you, Keylan."

"You're welcome. Try them on," he suggested.

"Okeydoke." Colby ran and plopped onto the sofa and started putting the shoes on his feet.

"What are you doing?" Mia asked, her tone sharp.

Keylan looked around the room. "You really aren't into Christmas. There's not one sign of the holiday, outside or in," he remarked, ignoring her question.

"No, I'm not…not all the unnecessary trappings, anyway. Now answer my question. What do you think you're doing?" she demanded.

"What do you mean?" Keylan's face scrunched up.

"Are you kidding right now? Why do you think he wears Velcro tennis shoes? They're not a fashion statement," she said with both hands on her hips, facing away from her son.

"Clearly." The corners of Keylan's mouth turned up as he looked past Mia.

Mia frowned, fighting the urge to smack that grin off his face. "Are you mocking me?"

Keylan sighed, took Mia by the shoulders and turned her toward Colby, who was now sitting on the floor tying his shoes. "Pull the bunny ears out. Yay me!" Colby cheered.

"Wh…what's he doing?" Mia murmured.

"I believe it's called tying his shoes," he whispered.

"That's not possible. Colby doesn't know how to tie his own shoes. He's not ready," she declared.

"You sure about that?"

"I'm positive. He's my son." She looked over her shoulder at him and repeated, "I know my son."

"Colby, let's show your mother what you can do." Keylan sat next to Colby on the floor and untied his own shoe.

"Wait, di…did you teach him…?" She couldn't make herself say the words.

Keylan smiled and winked at her. "And you thought all we do is play when we're hanging out."

"I…"

"Ready?" Keylan asked Colby.

"Ready," Colby said excitedly. "Watch, Mommy."

Mia was overwhelmed by emotions. She had tried to teach Colby to tie his shoes to no avail but now, thanks to Keylan, her son could actually do it. "I'm watching, little man," she said, brushing away her tears.

Mia turned and stared at Colby, her face blank. "You will eat some of your salad, young man."

Colby dropped his arms and said, "Okeydoke, Mommy."

"Wow, that was a real mom-like moment."

"What did you expect? I am a mother." Mia retrieved the salad from the refrigerator and placed some in each bowl.

That you are. Keylan rose from his chair. "Isn't there anything we can do to help?"

"Well, Colby can get his dinner wrap out and you can help him put it on," she instructed as she prepared another pan to grill their buns, toasting Colby's. "Is two good?"

"Two what?" Keylan questioned as he watched the way Mia moved around the kitchen so effortlessly, loading the dishwasher as she went.

"I'll get the wrap, Mommy."

"Thanks, son. Two sloppy Joes," she answered.

"Sure." Keylan smiled at the joy that suddenly came over Colby's face. He clearly enjoyed helping his mother.

"Colby, your usual three?"

"Yep," he replied, handing Keylan a folded cloth before returning to his chair.

"Three? You have a big appetite," Keylan replied, examining the cloth he held. "What is this?"

"My wrap. It's for my mess," Colby said, sitting straighter in his chair.

"Just snap it around his neck," Mia instructed her guest.

Keylan unfolded the wrap and placed it over Colby, covering the front part of his whole body, snapping it at his neck. *This is a giant bib.*

"Thank you," Colby replied.

"He wears this every time he eats?" Keylan asked, frowning.

"Usually," Mia replied, flipping the buns onto a platter and turning off the stove burner.

"Why?" he murmured to himself.

"It protects his clothes from mess."

"But he's supposed to make messes. He's a four-year-old boy."

Mia laughed. "Is that a rule or something?"

"If it isn't, it should be," Keylan mumbled. His mind flashed back to all the proper and clean dinners he and his mother had had when he was Colby's age.

Mia placed meat on three mini and three large buns. She handed the plate of minis to Colby. "Here you go, little man."

Colby smiled up at his mother as he accepted his plate. "I'm going to need about twenty of those," Keylan said.

Mia smiled, turned back to her counter and retrieved two more plates: one with two large burgers, the other with a single. "Well, we have plenty, but how about we start with these?" She handed Keylan his plate and smiled.

"Thank you, this looks and smells great."

"You're welcome. It's just one of our quick Saturday night meals before movie time."

"Grace, Mommy," Colby reminded her, placing his palms together.

"I know." Mia and Keylan bowed their heads as Colby led them in a short grace that he ended with "Let's eat," which they did.

Keylan ate as he listened to Colby dominate the conversation with his version of what had happened at the bowling alley earlier in the day. Mia threw her head back and laughed at Colby's impersonation of how his uncle Rudy and Keylan had acted at losing to him at Skee-Ball.

His body stirred at the sound, at the loving way she ran her hand through Colby's hair and the teasing looks she gave him. He was struggling to keep control because no matter what he'd said to anyone before, Keylan wanted Mia.

Colby's bowling story was one of many embarrassing ones he shared that Keylan denied between bites and bits of laughter. He also noticed that Colby not only ate most of his salad, but drank two juice boxes, ate all three burgers and hadn't dropped an ounce on his "wrap," as Mia insisted on calling it.

"All done?" Mia asked Colby.

"Yep."

"Why don't you go wash your hands and pick out the movie?"

"Will do." Colby pulled off his wrap, jumped down and ran out of the room.

"That's a great kid you got there. Although you really should talk to him about his tendency to exaggerate. He didn't beat me at Skee-Ball. I just didn't win."

Mia laughed. "Oh, really?"

"Really." Keylan picked up a napkin, moved to the seat now abandoned by Colby, leaned in and wiped some sauce from the corner of Mia's mouth.

"Thanks. Did you get it all?" Mia used her tongue to circle her lips. It was a move that sent Keylan's body into a frenzy and he lost all control. He captured her face with both hands and devoured her mouth. It was a kiss of pure desperation. He pulled and sucked her tongue and lips as if his life depended on it. Just as quickly as he'd taken her, he forced himself to stop.

"I'm sorry," he said, leaning away from her.

"Why?" she whispered, bringing her left hand to her lips.

"I probably should have taken it a little slower or at least asked."

"Permission granted," she whispered.

Keylan watched as her breasts rose and fell quickly and he could see the desire in her eyes. He was sure it couldn't compare to his own. He leaned forward when Colby announced, "Got one."

Mia and Keylan turned to find Colby had changed out of his clothes and was now wearing his pj's, waving his favorite superhero movie in the air.

"Nice pj's, man," Keylan observed.

"Thank you. Mommy bought them."

"Colby, I'm not sure Keylan has time for a movie, too."

You're not getting rid of me that easily. "I sure do. I have all evening," he explained, his eyes jumping from Colby to Mia. "All evening."

"In that case, why don't you two go start the movie while I tidy up in here?"

"Yay." Colby ran from the room.

Keylan stood, leaned down and passionately kissed her on the lips before leaving a trail behind him as he made his way to her right ear, where he whispered, "Don't take too long. Our evening is far from over." Keylan straightened to his full height and went to join Colby in the living room.

Chapter 14

Mia stood at her island, trying to calm herself. "What the hell was that?" Mia shook her head as if she needed to wake up from some dream. "That was the most incredible kiss you ever had, is what that was. It was just a kiss. He kisses lots of women like that, I'm sure. You're probably in this by yourself. So get it together and stop talking to yourself."

She moved to her pantry, pulled out a package of popcorn and placed it in the microwave. Mia finished cleaning her kitchen while waiting for the popcorn to get ready. After retrieving two bottles of beer and a water for Colby from the refrigerator, the microwave stopped. Mia removed the hot pouch and emptied its kettle-flavored contents into a bowl. She dropped the trash in the can, grabbed a few napkins and placed everything on a serving tray. "It's just a movie," she repeated as she walked into the living room.

"Popcorn!" Colby cheered.

"Let me get that," Keylan said as he rose from his place on the sofa.

"Sit here, Mommy," Colby instructed, patting the empty space between him and Keylan.

Mia smiled at her son. If she didn't know any better, she'd think he was playing matchmaker. She sat as instructed and accepted the throw blanket that she usually wrapped herself in, which was now being shared by her extremely handsome visitor.

"Shouldn't you change that dressing?" he asked, glancing at her hand.

"I will…later," she said.

"Popcorn, please." Colby held out his hand.

Keylan picked up the bowl and passed it to Colby.

He then twisted the tops off both beers before handing one to Mia. He raised his bottle and said, "To an amazing day." He tapped his bottle against hers.

"An amazing day."

Keylan took a drink from his bottle, sat back and stretched out his left arm, resting it on the back of the sofa. Mia sat straight as she sipped her beer. "Sit back, Mommy. I wanna lie down."

Mia glanced over at Keylan, who gave her a wolfish grin. If this wasn't their normal practice, watching the movie while Colby laid his head on her lap, she'd know these two were in cahoots. Mia sighed, placed her bottle on the table and sat back. Colby smiled at them both before laying his head on his favorite human pillow.

"Much better," Keylan said before bringing his arm down, placing it around her shoulders.

Easy for you to say. Mia was overwhelmed by all the emotions she was experiencing. Desire was one thing that she could handle. This was something else…a feeling of security, trust…family. Mia felt Keylan's hand rise from her shoulder and land in her hair, where he removed the clip and placed it on the small table that sat behind the sofa, allowing Mia's hair to fall free.

"What are you doing?" she whispered, trying not to disturb Colby, who had his eyes closed.

"I prefer it this way. Do you have a problem with that?" he asked, running his fingers through her curls.

"No," she uttered, looking up into his passion-filled eyes. She raised her chin, offering herself to him, and Keylan didn't hesitate.

Keylan leaned down and kissed her gently on the lips. He cupped Mia's face with his right hand and the kiss became more passionate. Colby stirred and Keylan dropped his hand and leaned his forehead against hers. Mia whispered, "I thought I was in this alone."

"Not hardly…"

"I better go put this little guy down. He falls asleep at the exact same spot in this movie."

"I'll take him." Keylan rose and picked up Mia's sleeping son. When he snuggled him in his arms, her heart melted. "Which way?"

"Down the hall to the left."

Mia followed Keylan into Colby's room. She laughed at the look on his face as he examined all the images that lay before him. "Wow, this kid sure has a thing for superheroes."

"I know," she replied, pulling back his covers.

He placed Colby on the bed. "Good night, little man." He leaned in and kissed him on the forehead.

Keylan stepped away from the bed and Mia sat next to her son. She ran her hand through his hair and said, "Sleep well, my little man. Mommy loves you." Mia kissed him on the cheek, rose and tucked him in. She followed Keylan out of the bedroom, closing the door slightly behind her.

They returned to the living room and Keylan's phone beeped, indicating he'd gotten a text message. He checked the screen before returning the phone to his pocket. "It's getting late. I should go."

"You sure you wouldn't like to stay a little while longer? It's barely ten."

"I think it's best if we call it a night," he said.

Mia lowered her head. "Okay," she replied, heading toward the door. She wanted to kick herself for sounding so pathetic.

Keylan reached for her hand, stopping her progress. "Mia, don't overthink this. I had a wonderful time and I'd like to see you again. How about you and Colby join me tomorrow afternoon at the opening of my pop-up shoe store?"

"Are you sure you won't be too busy?" Mia was trying to hold back her excitement.

"For you two, never," he promised before leaning down and capturing her mouth in a mind-melting kiss. "We're in this together."

Mia smiled. "Okay." She walked him to the door and said good-night. Mia looked at the cleaning that needed to be done and decided she needed a shower first...a cold one.

Keylan drove the relatively short distance to his apartment. He parked near the front entrance and walked into his building's lobby. He was greeted by his nervous-looking doorman. "Good evening, Mr. Kingsley. I'm sorry I had to bother you but I figured you'd want to know if someone was going into your apartment, no matter who it was."

"Thanks, and you did the right thing. How long has she been here?"

"They arrived about thirty minutes ago," he informed him.

"'They'?" Keylan frowned.

"She had her key and Ms. Bella was with her. I hope that was okay."

Keylan sighed. "It was, and you didn't need to do anything more."

He walked to the private elevator. After inserting his access card into the security pad, the doors opened. He hit the button to the top floor and, after a brief ride, the elevator opened to the short distance that led to his front door. Keylan pulled out a different card key, ran it over his electronic lock and opened his door. He took a deep breath and released it slowly before crossing the threshold.

He entered the apartment, closing the door behind him. The room was dimly lit. The only light fighting against the darkness was that from the city skyline shining through the wall of windows that led out to his balcony. "Lights on," he ordered. His eyes scanned the room until he found his target.

He walked over to his sunken living room, surveyed the area and shook his head. Two beautiful women, clearly dressed for a night of partying, were asleep on his sofas. There was one electric cigarette, two pink wigs, an empty bottle of Don Julio 1942 tequila and two shot glasses sitting on his coffee table. "Some smart house you are. You let these two in and allowed them to finish off my tequila," he chastised the quiet room.

He walked to the closet next to the door and pulled out two light blankets from the top shelf. Keylan returned to his unexpected guests and covered them both. He walked into the kitchen, removed two bottles of water from the refrigerator, reached into a nearby cabinet and pulled down a bottle of aspirin. He returned to the living room and placed everything on the coffee table and said, "Sleep well, ladies. Lights off."

Keylan walked down the hall and into his bedroom. "Lights on." His extra-wide and long bed sat against a wood-planked wall, which, acting as both a headboard and decorative piece, dominated the room. The bed could sleep six people comfortably and was the crown jewel of his apartment. Not even the city's view from his wraparound balcony could compete with it.

After emptying his pocket contents onto a silver tray that

sat on the dresser, Keylan removed his Hublot Big Bang Ferrari watch and placed it into an oscillating box. "Blinds close," he said as he picked up his phone, hit two numbers and listened for the call to connect.

"Good evening, sir."

"Good evening. Well…?"

"All's quiet here. Shortly after you left, the house went mostly dark. There were a couple of cars that circled the block and we ran their plates."

"And?"

"Paparazzi. After they realized you weren't here, they left."

"Great. Is everything set for tomorrow?"

"Yes, sir."

"Good. Now tell me how these two ended up in my apartment and you better warn your bosses, because when my mother and Aunt Elizabeth find out, there *will* be hell to pay."

After receiving a full report from his security, Keylan changed into his workout clothes, walked down the hall to his home gym and put himself through a grueling work-out. However, no matter how hard he punched and kicked his boxing bag or how many push-ups and sit-ups he did, his body was screaming for a release that only Mia could satisfy. He pushed himself until he was exhausted.

Keylan returned to his bedroom and walked into his large bathroom. "Shower on." He undressed and dropped his clothes in the hamper before walking into a shower that could hold several people at once. He stepped under the contemporary rain showerhead, raised his head, closed his eyes and enjoyed all sprays that punched his body. After fifteen minutes, emerging more relaxed and exhausted, he dried off and climbed into bed, forgoing clothes.

Keylan rolled onto his back and stretched out his arms,

realizing immediately he was not alone. He opened his eyes and sat up.

"Good morning. So, who is Mia? You called out her name a couple of times in your sleep," asked a short-haired beauty wearing his robe, drinking a cup of coffee and sitting next to him on the bed.

The only woman I want in my bed. Keylan ran his hands down his face and through his hair. The last thing he wanted was to have to deal with his ex-girlfriend and unwelcome houseguest, wealthy socialite Bella Weatherspoon. "What are you doing here, Bella?"

"I came with your cousin Kristen. Want some?" she said, offering him a wicked smile and her cup.

Kristen Kingsley was Aunt Elizabeth's eldest child and vice president of operations for Kingsley Oil and Gas.

He could see she was offering him more than her coffee. "No thanks, I'll get my own. I'm asking why you are in my bedroom."

"Well—" she sipped her coffee, eyeing him over her cup "—I thought you might like a little Sunday morning loving, since your cousin is sound asleep."

"No, I'm good."

She offered a sly smile. "Oh, really?" Bella pulled back his covers, exposing his naked and erect body. Her eyes zeroed in on his sex. "I can help you with that, you know."

"No, thanks. Shouldn't you be getting dressed so you can go?" Keylan got out of bed and headed to his bathroom.

Bella put her cup on his nightstand and blocked his path. "You sure about that?" She opened the robe, exposing her naked body. "You know you want to," she declared, reaching for him.

Keylan couldn't deny how beautiful and desirable Bella was, but all he could think about was Mia.

He blocked her hand and took a step back. "No, I don't."
Bella closed the robe and crossed her arms. "Mia?"
"Mia." He walked around Bella and into his bathroom.

Chapter 15

Mia stood at the kitchen sink with her aunt as they washed the Sunday brunch dishes. While she might not have been big on the Christmas season, her aunt certainly was. Since last week's visit, their three-bedroom, traditional-decorated cottage had turned into a winter wonderland all centered around a nine-foot frosted Christmas tree placed in the corner of the room.

"Aunt Mavis, why do you insist on washing your dishes before you load them in the dishwasher?" she asked, accepting the pan she'd just washed and placing it in the dishwasher.

"That thing is only good for sanitation and drying," she declared.

"Oh…okay." Mia shook her head.

"So, how was your date?" her aunt asked, smiling.

"It wasn't—"

"Child, please." Her aunt gave her the side-eye.

Mia dropped her shoulders. "Maybe it was a date. It was fine."

"Just fine." Mavis gave a lopsided sneer.

A smile crept across Mia's face. "It was great. Colby had a blast."

"Well, it's pretty clear that he's crazy about Colby, but I'm asking how things between the two of you are."

"It was nice. He was sweet." Mia bit her lip as images of the passionate kisses they'd shared and the hopeful words he'd said flooded her mind.

"Your face is flushed. That tells me your night was more than just nice and sweet. I should know. I'm always flushed after quality sexy time," she bragged.

Mia looked over her shoulder into the family room off the kitchen to ensure they weren't overheard by Colby. "First, eww. Second, there was no 'sexy time' to be had."

"Too bad."

Mia's eyes widened with surprise, although she wasn't sure why. She was used to her aunt's unfiltered opinions. "Auntie, it was our first date."

"Oh, please," her aunt said, offering a nonchalant wave. "Sexy time doesn't have to include penetration, you know."

Mia raised her hands. "I'm not having this conversation with you."

"Fine. When are you seeing him again?" Mavis asked, drying her hands and starting the dishwasher.

Mia checked the clock on the wall. "In about an hour and a half."

"Really?"

"He invited us to the grand opening of his shoe pop-up shop this afternoon."

Mavis took a seat at the kitchen table. "That's wonderful—"

"I'm think about canceling," she informed her, pouring herself a cup of coffee before joining her aunt at the table.

"Why in the world would you do that?"

"We're just so different." Mia sipped her coffee.

"Different can be good."

"Not always. We wouldn't even be doing whatever it is

we're doing if he hadn't been forced to do community service by the league."

"You don't know that, Mia." Her aunt reached across the table and squeezed her hand.

"Oh, but I do. You know how many events I've planned for his family over the years? Way too many to count, and you know how many he actually attended?"

"No."

"Less than I could count on one hand," she stated.

"Sweetheart, he plays in the NBA."

"And there is that, too."

"What does—?"

"Not to mention his obsession with helping me find my 'Christmas mojo,' as he puts it," Mia said, ignoring her aunt's shaking her head. "All because I don't celebrate the way he thinks I should."

"Well, you could put up a light or two...especially since yours is the only house on your block not decorated."

Mia rose and placed her coffee cup in the sink. "Not you, too?"

"You used to love decorating for the holidays when you were a kid, even after my sister flaked."

"That's because you and Uncle Rudy always made it such an event." Mia glanced over at her uncle, who was reading a Christmas story to Colby.

"And you should do the same for Colby."

"He's four and he doesn't really get it. Anyway, he doesn't like the big moving yard decorations. They scare him."

"That's because you haven't explained it to him, and you don't have to get those types of yard decorations. He seems to like our decorations and the ones at the foundation."

"Mommy, I wanna see Keylan," he yelled out from the living room.

Mia checked the time on her watch. "Shoot, I guess it's too late to cancel now."

"It would be terribly rude if you did and I certainly taught you better than that," her aunt said with a smug look on her face.

"Funny, very funny."

Dressed in jeans, a black button-down shirt and wearing his new black signature sneakers, Keylan walked into his kitchen to find his cousin Kristen wearing one of his T-shirts that fit her small frame like a dress. She was standing in front of his stove scrambling eggs while Bella sat at the island, still wearing his robe, flipping through her cell phone.

"Good morning, ladies." Keylan reached into the cabinet for a coffee mug. "Kristen, I gave you a key to my place for emergencies."

"Morning, cousin," Kristen responded while Bella remained silent, keeping her eyes on her phone.

Keylan reached for the coffeepot and poured himself a cup. "Which one of you would like to explain what the hell happened last night?"

"There's nothing to tell," Kristen said as she placed eggs on three plates.

"There sure as hell is when you ditch your security, get drunk and pass out on my sofa." His voice was hard.

"It was no big deal, Keylan," Bella quipped, accepting the plate Kristen offered.

"It's a very big deal, Bella," he seethed, glaring over at her before turning his attention back to Kristen. "And you know better. So I'll ask again. What happened last night?"

"I was…sad about breaking up with James and needed to blow off some steam," Kristen explained.

"And I offered to cheer her up. We wanted to bar hop

but couldn't with all the security y'all travel with, so we ditched them."

He frowned as his eyes darted between the two women before landing on his cousin. "You do know how stupid and reckless that was, right?" he asked Kristen.

"It was fine. No one recognized me. I wore a wig," she said before biting into her food.

"A pink one," Bella added.

"This is not fine. This is far from fine. You're a vice president for a multibillion-dollar company that's under siege by both known and unknown enemies. You can't just ditch your security detail whenever you feel like it."

"Why not? You did it all the time," she reminded him.

"Yeah, well, we were kids. You're not a kid anymore. This is a dangerous time for us all."

"Don't you think I know that!" she snapped back, rising from her seat and dropping her plate in the sink. "Between the EPA's investigation, threats of another one coming from OSHA and maybe even the IRS, not to mention concerns of physical threats, I just needed a moment to not be a Kingsley."

Keylan's shoulders dropped. He knew exactly how difficult it was being a Kingsley, not to mention the toll it took on relationships. While he questioned his choice to bring Mia and her son into his world, he felt he had no real choice. He wanted them.

"I get that, but you can't ditch your protection. I know the added level of security and all the scrutiny it brings is a pain, but until things get back to normal—"

"Whatever normal is in this family," she grunted, her annoyance clear.

Keylan nodded. "You'll just have to go along with these changes for now. We all do. I'm sorry about James."

Kristen gave a nonchalant shrug. "He wasn't The One. I

just hope when and if he ever shows up, our lifestyle won't mess things up."

"Me, too," he murmured, pulling her into his arms when the doorbell rang. "Can you get that, Bella? It's Rivers and his team."

The toaster popped. "I guess." She rose and headed for the door. "Don't touch my Pop-Tarts."

"You might want to put some clothes on, too," he yelled after her. "That goes for you, too." He released Kristen.

"Keylan, darling, it's not Rivers," Bella yelled out.

Keylan checked his watch. "Dammit!" He ran to the door.

"Mia…Colby, you're right on time," Keylan said, stopping short at the sight before him. Mia was standing in the doorway, her expression closed off and her complexion lacking color, while Colby held tight to his mother's hand and waist.

Keylan was suddenly haunted by the thought that anything that he and Mia might have had could be ruined or even tainted by a misunderstanding. He knew he had to act quickly.

"Kristen, get out here…now!" he demanded; panic was setting in.

Colby squeezed his mother's waist and hid his face in her side.

Keylan's heart dropped.

"We should go," Mia said.

"Please wait. I can explain all of this." His voice had taken on a calming tone.

"What, you told me to get dressed. Oh, Mia, how are you?" Her shock at Mia's presence was written all over his cousin's face.

"She's not doing well at the moment," Keylan responded on her behalf. "Please tell her what's going on here."

Kristen's brows drew together as she gave everyone the once-over, clearly assessing the situation. "Yes, of course. Mia, this is my friend Bella—"

"And Keylan's ex-girlfriend," Bella chimed in.

"Yes, and there hasn't been anything between us in over three years," Keylan explained.

"Unfortunately that's true, too," Bella conceded before turning to leave the room.

"Anyway, Bella and I partied a little too hard last night and ended up crashing here…on the couch." She pointed to the supporting evidence in the sunken area of his living room.

Keylan watched as the color slowly returned to Mia's face. His eyes darted to his cousin and he held her gaze for several seconds before dropping them down to Colby. He was hoping she could read his expression and give him the time he needed.

Kristen smiled at Colby. "Hey, little man." She stooped down. "Remember me? I come to see you and your mother at your office from time to time."

Colby nodded, released his mother's hand and offered Kristen a quick wave.

"If it's okay with your mom, how would you like some hot chocolate?"

"I like hot chocolate," he said, stepping away from his mother. "Got marshmallows?"

"Sure do." Kristen looked up at Mia. "Would it be okay if we go have a cup while you two talk?"

"Please, Mommy."

Mia smiled and nodded. "Sure," she said.

Kristen rose, took Colby's hand and led him out of the room and into the kitchen.

"Thank you for not just taking Colby and leaving. I know it couldn't have been easy." Keylan took her hands and intertwined their fingers. "I can just imagine how you must've felt and what went through your mind when Bella opened the door dressed in my robe."

Mia tilted her head and frowned. "Can you?"

Chapter 16

Mia's mind took the short leap back to the last twenty minutes.

"Come on, Mommy," Colby had said, pulling Mia's hand and moving toward the security desk in the lobby of Keylan's high-rise apartment building. His excitement was hard to contain.

"Good afternoon. May I help you?" the security officer had asked, putting down the newspaper he'd been reading.

"Yes, I'm here to see Keylan Kingsley. I'm Mia Ramirez."

The security officer checked his tablet. "Yes, ma'am, follow me." The officer had led them to a private elevator, used his access card to open the doors and gestured for them to enter. He'd hit the button marked P and said, "His apartment is P1. You'll see it as soon as you exit the elevator."

"Thank you," Mia had replied. Her own excitement grew with each floor they passed. She'd checked her reflection in the mirrored walls and the corner of her mouth rose. Mia had struggled with deciding what to wear but now she was happy she selected the red-and-black formfitting dress that showed off how physically fit she was. Her red Christian Louboutin shoes gave her the extra five inches of confidence she needed.

"You're so pretty, Mommy," Colby said.

"Thank you, son—you're pretty handsome yourself." Colby had insisted on wearing his jeans and a T-shirt with Keylan's number on it, which he'd paired with the new *sneakers* Keylan had given him.

The elevator door had stopped and so had Mia's heart for about two seconds. "We're here," Colby yelled.

"Yes, we are," Mia mumbled as the elevator door opened.

They exited into a brightly lit hall and, as promised, the door with P1 on it was less than ten feet away from them. They'd walked up to the door; Mia had raised her left hand to knock and suddenly she couldn't do it. She looked down at Colby, who was squirming and trying to pull his hand free from hers, and she knew she had come too far now. She had let this man invade her life…their lives and, more importantly, their hearts. Now her only hope was that it wasn't a mistake. Mia dropped her hand and had said, "Why don't you ring the bell, son, just once?"

"Okay." Colby happily complied.

The door opened and Mia's heart had dropped. She'd looked down at the floor as if she needed to make sure it hadn't actually left her body. Mia felt Colby squeeze her hand like he always did when he was faced with a stranger or an uncomfortable situation. The tall, beautiful woman wearing a black robe with the letters *KJ* monogrammed in gold on its pockets would definitely fall into the category of an uncomfortable situation.

"May I help you?" the woman had asked, her annoyance coming through loud and clear.

Mia was sure she'd interrupted something and all she'd wanted to do was make a fast exit. However, before she could get the word *no* past her lips, Colby had said, "I want to see Keylan."

Mia's eyes dropped to her son. She couldn't believe

now was the moment he'd decided to be brave and asser- tive. This was something else Keylan had taught him. Mia looked back at the woman but couldn't get her mouth to work. When she'd heard the woman call out for Keylan, Mia thought she'd be sick on the spot.

She didn't know what to do or say when Keylan ap- peared fully dressed with a smile that quickly morphed into something that looked like fear. The next few minutes had been a haze of emotions she'd tried to fight through. Mia heard everyone's explanation for the presence of the woman she now knew was Bella, but she was still strug- gling to make her mouth work as her brain and heart were in a tug-of-war. Should she leave or stay? It was Colby's "Please, Mommy," that broke the tie.

"Really?" she asked Keylan now, wishing she could get those last several minutes back.

"Of course." He brought her hands to his mouth and kissed them.

"That's interesting," she replied, pulling her hands from his. "Because I just experienced an explosion of emotions that I'm still struggling to understand."

Mia tried to step away from Keylan; only he blocked her path. "Wait, what I meant was I know how I felt when I thought I might have hurt you…maybe even lost you over something that didn't happen."

Mia lowered her head and slowly shook it as tears stung the backs of her eyes. She whispered, "You're not supposed to be here."

Keylan used his right index finger to raise her head and he stared into her eyes. "Where am I not supposed to be?"

Mia took his hand and placed it over her heart. "Here."

Keylan pulled Mia into his arms and kissed her pas- sionately on the lips. It was the type of kiss that demanded more, a fact that the lower part of his body was making clear to Mia.

"You're blocking my exit," Bella announced, her voice hard.

Mia tried to step out of Keylan's arms but he held on to her. "Sorry," he said, adjusting them to get out of the way.

"Whatever." Bella sashayed through the door, slamming it on her way out.

Mia knew it wasn't right but she felt a sense of satisfaction at her exit. "That was—"

"Something that's been over for quite some time."

"Excuse me, guys." Kristen interrupted with a big smile on her face. "Colby's almost done and, Keylan, you have to get to your soft opening."

"Look who's back in work mode." Keylan checked his watch. "It's not like they can start without me."

"True, but do you really want to have to deal with your mother, too? She's already going to be pissed about last night, which of course I'll blame on you."

"On me?" Keylan's eyebrows came together.

"Yes, you. Who do you think I got my rebellious streak from?"

"My mother, since you certainly didn't get it from yours," he replied matter-of-factly.

"True, but it's not like I can blame her for this," she replied, laughing.

"I'm finished," Colby announced, whipped cream all over his face.

Everyone laughed. "Let's clean you up so we can go," Keylan said.

"Are you sure it's a good idea for us to be there with you?" Mia asked.

"It doesn't matter." Keylan cupped Mia's face with his right hand and ran his thumb across her lips. "It's what I want...what I need." He then took Colby's hand and led him back into the kitchen.

Kristen's smile widened. "You're in trouble now."

"What are you talking about?"

"The only time I've seen that look on Keylan's face or heard him confess that he needed something was when he decided he had to go to a public high school so he could start working toward his goal of going to the NBA."

"Really?" Mia could feel the warmth growing inside her.

"Really. Keylan has set his eyes on you and Colby. You're as good as got and I think it's great, too."

"What if I don't want to be got?" Mia could hardly get those words past her lips. The bitter aftertaste made her nose crinkle.

Kristen laughed. "Girl, he's already got you. He just doesn't know it yet."

"I'm ready," said a clean-faced Colby, running up to Mia.

Keylan came and stood by them both. He ran his left hand through Colby's hair while taking Mia's hand with his right. "Ready, baby?"

Mia's eyes cut to Kristen, who offered her an encouraging nod. "I'm ready."

"We'll take your vehicle since I don't have a booster seat yet, but I'll drive."

Yet?

The short drive from Keylan's apartment to the upscale Galleria mall was filled with laughter and pleasant conversation between Keylan and Colby. Mia was astonished by the level of genuine interest Keylan showed Colby, even when he would ask the simplest of questions.

Keylan held both their hands as they entered the mall from the underground level where he had parked. They were met by a tall, brown-skinned man wearing an expensive suit.

"There you are," he said in greeting.

Keylan introduced him. "Mia, Colby, this is my agent, Roger."

"Hi," Mia replied and Colby waved.

Roger nodded. "Nice to meet you both."

"Everything ready?" Keylan asked as he silenced his ringing phone.

"Yep, and there's more press than we initially expected. Speaking of unexpected…"

"What?" Keylan glared at Roger.

"You know how we planned for five hundred people to showcase the shoes to?" Roger looked nervous.

"Yes." Keylan's eyes narrowed.

"Well, there's a thousand or so people in the space and a few more thousand waiting outside the shop to see you," Roger explained.

Keylan's face went blank. "I figured as much. Did you bring them?"

"Yes, but I'm not sure why you need them." Roger placed a small package in his hand.

Mia's heart sped up as she looked at her son. "Keylan, I think we should—"

"No, I want you both with me."

He knelt and looked into Colby's eyes. "Little man, when you go inside, there's going to be a lot of people and lots of noise. I want you to wear these and stay close to me and your mom." He placed a pair of earplugs in Colby's ears. "Is that okay?"

Colby smiled and said, "It's okay." His voice rose an octave.

Keylan stood and turned back to Mia. "Ready?"

"Absolutely." Mia was overflowing with joy by Keylan's

kind and thoughtful gesture. Not to mention all the other emotions he had provoked. Now all she had to do was figure out what she wanted to do about them.

Chapter 17

Mia spent the next hour sitting at a small table that had been set up for her and Colby. She watched over her son, who was happily playing games on a tablet Keylan had commandeered for his use. Mia still couldn't believe all the special arrangements Keylan had made to ensure Colby would be comfortable. Even though he was busy signing shoes and taking pictures, she often caught him looking over at them as though he was making sure they were still there. His smile sent her heart racing.

"Excuse me, I'm Ryan from the *Houston Sentinel*. I couldn't help but notice the way KJ keeps eyeing you and the boy. Are you two together? Wasn't that you that KJ was with at the clinic yesterday? Why were you there?" He shot questions at her like she was a dartboard before he raised his camera and started taking her picture.

"Please leave us alone," she replied, rising from her chair and stepping slightly away from the table, blocking his view of her son.

"You, KJ and the kid, what's the deal?" He took another picture; only he aimed his camera at Colby.

"Please stop taking pictures of us," she demanded, turning her back to him.

"Hold up," he ordered, grabbing her arm.

Before Mia could respond, Keylan appeared, capturing the man by the neck. "Let go of my girl's arm before I snap your damn neck."

"Keylan," Mia murmured, pushing back her fear and keeping an eye on her son.

The room was still for about ten seconds before lights began flashing in their faces and questions were being shouted out at them. Roger and another large man appeared and stepped between Keylan and the reporter.

"Keylan, let the man go," Roger insisted, pulling at his hand. "You don't want to do this here."

"Like hell," he replied. Rage had transformed Keylan's face and it was on full display.

"We got this, sir," the larger man reassured Keylan, tapping him on the shoulder.

Keylan dropped his hands and fisted them at his sides.

"Clear this place and close the doors," Roger ordered the curious sales team.

Keylan turn to Mia and asked, "Are you okay, baby?"

Mia nodded and stepped into his outspread arms. "I am now."

"Sorry about that," he whispered. Keylan glanced over at the small table where Colby had been sitting just as his cell phone rang. It was a familiar ring that he knew he had to answer. "Where's Colby?"

Mia turned in Keylan's arms and stared at the spot where her son had just been. The earbuds were sitting on the table next to the tablet. Mia's heart sank and she began trembling all over. She was so gripped by fear that she couldn't make out a word Keylan had just said. He turned her toward him and repeated, "Colby's fine."

"Wh-what?"

"That was my security team calling—they have him.

He wandered off during all the commotion. He's two doors down."

"Thank God. Wait, what?" She scowled. "You have a security team?"

"This way." They left the store and walked the two doors down to find Colby standing in front of a boutique with a small Christmas tree sitting just inside the entrance. The tree was Colby's height and looked like it had been on a severe diet. The colorful lights wrapped around the tree were blinking to the tune of "Jingle Bells."

"Colby," Mia called out. She was drowning in relief at the sight of him.

"Look, Mommy," he said, pointing to the tree while he swayed and sang along with the song. The look of pure joy on her son's face allowed her to push past the lump in her throat.

"Wow, that tree is something else," Keylan commented with a confused look on his face.

Mia giggled and then said, "It's a Charlie Brown tree."

"Oh…okay."

"Excuse me, KJ…can I talk to you for a minute?" Roger asked.

"Sure, but you can talk in front of Mia," Keylan instructed.

"That little outburst back there is all over the net. It'll for sure be on the news tonight, too."

"What?" Mia's face went blank.

"It'll be fine. It's not that big of a deal." Keylan gave a nonchalant shrug.

"It most certainly is, Keylan. I don't want our names and faces—" she looked over at her son "—splattered all over the news."

"Keylan, tree," Colby yelled.

"I see, little man. You like that tree."

"Yes, tree sings." Colby gifted them with a toothy smile.

Keylan looked down at Mia. "Everything's going be fine." He turned to Colby and said, "Since you were such a brave boy today, and if it's okay with your mom, how would you like to have that tree?"

Colby nodded. "Can I have the tree?"

"You most certainly can," he promised.

"Keylan, you just can't promise him that tree. It may not even be for sale," Mia scolded.

"It's a department store. Everything's for sale. Besides, didn't you tell me he didn't really like trees? Well, he obviously likes this one, so he should have it."

"I said he didn't like things that moved," she corrected, placing her hand on her hip.

"Well, this tree certainly doesn't move."

Mia watched as Keylan walked into the store and spoke to the salesperson for several minutes. He glanced at the little tree and around the store before handing her a wad of cash along with what looked like a business card. Keylan exited the store, squatted in front of Colby and said, "All right, buddy, I bought you the tree and I'm having it delivered to your house."

"Yeah…"

"What do you say, son?" Mia prompted.

"Thank you, Keylan." Colby hugged his neck and Mia felt a strong sense of family at the sight. It scared the hell out of her.

Keylan stood and took Colby's hand in his. "How about we get out of here?" he asked Mia, using his free hand to bring hers to his mouth, where he kissed her palm.

The feel of his lips and tongue on her hand sent waves of desire throughout her body. "Okay," she whispered.

Keylan's phone beeped twice; he dropped Mia's hand and pulled out his phone. He read the message and sighed.

"I'm sorry. My mother has called an emergency family meeting. How about I meet you at your place later? I can even bring dinner."

Mia fought back her disappointment. "Sure, but I'll cook. Do you need me to drop you off somewhere?"

"No, my security will take me to my car," he explained.

"About that security—"

"We'll talk about it, and anything else you like, this evening. The tree, along with a few other things I've ordered, will be delivered in a couple of hours."

"A few other things…what things?" Mia frowned.

Keylan ignored her question, picked up Colby and spun him around twice before holding him in his arms. "I have to leave for a while but I'll be back later. I promise."

"Okay." Colby giggled as Keylan tickled and kissed him on the cheek before placing him back on his feet.

Mia noticed how natural it seemed for Keylan to make promises and show affection toward her son, which only made the feelings she'd been trying to fight all that more difficult to ignore.

He turned to Mia. "Your turn."

"Are you going to spin me around, too?" She smiled up at him.

"Later." Keylan pulled her into his arms and gave her a sweet but not so quick kiss. He released her and whispered, "I have something much better planned for us later."

A sweet sensation made its way through her body, like a cure for something she'd been missing for far too long. It was difficult for her to step away from him. Mia couldn't believe it when she whispered, "Promise."

Keylan held her gaze and gave her another kiss before saying, "I promise, baby."

Keylan waved over Roger, who had been standing by, quietly watching. "I need you to make sure Mia and Colby get back to the car safely, understand?" He spoke in a commanding tone Mia never heard before and, by the look on Roger's face, neither had he.

"Yes, sir," Roger assured him.

As she watched Keylan walk away with his security team, the realization of just how much she didn't know about him hit her. She also realized that she wanted to know every single thing, too.

Mia arrived at her house to find Sandra walking up to her door. She pulled into her garage. They exited the vehicle and went to stare at the portable basketball hoop that was now placed in front of the left side of her driveway. Colby was so excited he could hardly contain himself. Mia wasn't sure if it was because there was a basketball hoop now in their driveway or because it had Keylan's picture on it.

"Since when have you been into basketball like this? Oh, wait, let me guess," Sandra teased, elbowing her friend in the side. "Since you became KJ's woman."

"What?" She turned and frowned at a grinning Sandra.

"Basketball hoop..." Keylan pointed at the backboard. "It's Keylan, Mommy."

"Yes, I see, son."

Mia turned back to Sandra. "What did you just call me?"

"Keylan's woman," she repeated.

"Let's get inside." Mia opened the door and Colby ran past her and down the hall to his bedroom. She dropped her purse and keys on the side table and walked into the living room, where she plopped down on the sofa. "Why did you call me that?"

"Seriously? KJ's proclamation is all over the net. Not to mention his barbaric yet heroic handling of that reporter." Sandra walked into the kitchen. "What smells so good? There's nothing on the stove and the oven isn't on."

Mia laid her head back on the sofa and closed her eyes. "There's a pot roast in the Crock-Pot."

Sandra walked over to the pot and raised the lid. "Mmm...that smells good."

"Yes, it does."

Colby ran back into the living room. "Mommy, I wanna go play basketball," he said, holding his ball under his arm.

Mia sat up in her seat. She could see the excitement radiating from her son's face. Before she could offer up an answer she knew would disappoint him, her doorbell rang.

"Hold that thought, little man," she said, rising from the sofa. She opened the door and smiled. "Roger, what are you doing here? Is everything okay?"

"Everything is fine. KJ wanted me to be here when his delivery arrived."

Mia smirked. "You're a little late. The basketball hoop was here when I got home."

"Not that delivery. This one." Roger stepped aside and Mia saw the reason Keylan had known his delivery would need an escort.

Chapter 18

Keylan walked into his mother's house, past her extravagantly decorated formal living and dining areas and a two-sided marble staircase, into a large family room adorned with blue and white contemporary furnishings. He found Travis walking through a side door that led from the casual dining and kitchen area, and his eldest brother, Alexander, standing in the middle of the living room.

"It's about time, little brother," Alexander, COO of Kingsley Oil and Gas, said, walking up to Keylan with his hand extended.

Keylan shook his brother's hand. "You sound like Mother. Where is she, anyway?"

"She'll be down in a bit. She had a few calls to return. How's the rehab going?"

"Good. I should be getting my release anytime now."

"When do you think you'll be getting back on the hardwood?"

"I'm waiting to hear from my agent. They're trying to get the commissioner to work out a deal about the suspension," Keylan explained.

"That was a bogus deal anyway," Travis remarked.

"Hopefully, I'll get in a few games before the year is out." Keylan felt encouraged.

"Cool," Alexander proclaimed.

"We figured you'd need one of these." Travis held three bottles of beer. He handed one to each brother before going to stand across the room from Keylan.

"Thanks." Keylan twisted off the top and took a long pull from his bottle.

Alexander checked and silenced his buzzing phone. "Before Mother joins us and starts in on the business update—"

"Wait, where is everyone else?" His brows drew together. Keylan was expecting his other brothers, as well as Kristen, although he'd had his fill of her today.

"Kristen is working on a special project for Mother, Morgan's out on one of the rigs and Brice is dealing with a personal issue," Alexander revealed.

"A personal issue? What kind of personal issue?" Keylan asked, frowning.

"The kind that he should've taken care of a long time ago, as far as I'm concerned, and that requires an attorney," Travis answered, taking a seat on the blue sofa.

"Oh…too bad," he remarked as Mia's face popped into his mind.

"Back to you." Alexander placed his beer on the coffee table.

Keylan sat on the white sofa, facing his cousin, while Alexander sat on the edge of one of two blue-and-white wingback chairs placed between the sofas, looking like a judge about to pass down a stiff sentence. "What about me?"

"You want to tell me about what happened today?" Alexander asked.

"Sounds like you already know," Keylan replied.

"Then tell me *why* it happened."

"That reporter crossed the line. He put his hands on Mia," Keylan informed him before taking another pull from his beer.

"I see…" Alexander picked up his beer and took a drink.

"Told you," Travis added.

Alexander nodded. "You were right."

"Right about what?" Keylan's eyes darted between his brother and his cousin.

"You're in love with Mia," Alexander pronounced matter-of-factly.

Keylan couldn't deny it, but he wasn't ready to admit it, either. Not out loud, anyway, and certainly not to these two. "I… I don't actually know what I am. I do know that I don't want to be without her, without them."

"Well, that's good to hear, because she's a package deal," Travis reminded him, his eyebrows standing at attention.

"I know, and I wouldn't have it any other way." Keylan leaned forward, resting his elbows on his knees. "I'm not just attracted to Mia. I care about her and her son. It kind of snuck up on me."

"I don't know why. You've always had a special place in your heart for special-needs kids. Not to mention beautiful women," Travis offered.

"Well, I'm happy for you. Now how about you let your security handle the takedowns from now on?" Alexander recommended.

"And chill out on the public service announcements in front of the press," Travis added.

All three men laughed. "I'll do my best," Keylan assured them.

"My apologies, children, my calls took longer than expected," Victoria announced as she entered the room in a long, short-sleeved blue dress, her hair pulled back in a tight bun.

All three Kingsley men stood. "Mother," Keylan and Alexander said in unison and kissed her on the cheek.

"Aunt Victoria." Travis came from across the room to offer the same greeting.

"Now that we're all here, we can get down to business." Victoria took the empty wingback chair next to Alexander.

Keylan checked his watch. "What's going on now, Mother?"

Victoria scowled at her son. "Someplace you have to be, or perhaps there is another *announcement* you'd like to make? Shall I call for a press conference?"

Keylan's face went blank. "I can explain."

Victoria raised her right hand. "I really don't care for the details and you know how I feel about drama, especially when it concerns my business. Just keep it off the damn news."

"This wasn't about business, Mother," he replied.

Victoria leaned forward and held her son's gaze. "You are my son. Everything you do is my business." She sat back in her seat.

"I told you," Travis murmured.

"Yes, ma'am," he replied, giving his cousin the evil eye.

"Now, back to business at hand. We've managed to hold off OSHA…for now."

"I still don't understand what workplace and health standards they think we violated," Travis said, stroking his chin.

"And we still can't prove for certain who's behind all this either." Alexander huffed.

"No, not yet, but we will. Now we hear the IRS wants to move up our annual reviews. I asked you here to explain how we plan to prepare for the IRS attack disguised as an audit. You know they'll be looking for the smallest of missteps to try to nail us on. To make sure that doesn't happen, I've decided to bring back our special consultant to work with Brice on the preparations," she announced.

"Are you serious?" Keylan said.

"Yes, very." Victoria rose and walked over to the bar, where she poured herself a glass of wine.

Travis's brows drew together. "Aunt Victoria, you don't mean Brooke—"

"Yes, of course, who else?" She took a sip of her wine.

"I know I'm not part of the day-to-day business but even I know how difficult that could be," Keylan attested.

"I agree, Aunt Victoria. There has to be someone else."

"There just might be, Travis…for some other company. Not ours or our family." Victoria returned to her chair. "For us, there's only one person, and she's family."

Keylan's phone beeped and he checked his messages. He smiled and typed out his response.

"Are we disturbing you, son?"

"Not at all. Besides, you've already made the decision."

Victoria crossed her legs. "That I have."

"We just have to make sure everything remains professional." Alexander rose from his chair. "I have to get back to China."

"How is she?" Travis asked.

"She and the baby are doing fine but I won't be if I don't get back with her dinner," Alexander said, leaning down to kiss his mother on the cheek.

"I can't wait to meet that little one. Do you know what you're having yet?" Travis inquired with a big smile on his face.

"No, China wants to be surprised." Alexander shrugged.

"Happy wife, as they say," Keylan said.

"Good night, son. Send China my love."

"Will do. Later, everyone." Alexander walked out of the house.

"I guess I should go, too, since I don't smell anything cooking," Travis teased Victoria.

"I'm your aunt, not your mother. However, I will take

you out for dinner. I'd hate for you to have to make that long trek back to your ranch on an empty stomach."

"Steaks?"

"What else?" Victoria frowned before her mouth curved into a big smile.

"You joining us, Keylan?" Travis stood and stretched out his arms.

"Not tonight. I have other plans."

"Of course you do." Travis collected the empty bottles and bumped elbows with Keylan before leaving to take the trash into the kitchen.

Victoria stood and walked her son to the door. "You know, Keylan, Mia and Colby are perfect for you. Just because I don't care about the drama doesn't mean I don't care about the outcome."

"I have to go home and change. Have a good evening, Mother." Keylan smiled and kissed his mother good-night.

"You, too, son."

Keylan had barely crossed his mother's threshold when his phone rang. He pulled out his phone as he made his way to the car. "You all right, man?" Keylan asked, knowing his friend and agent had taken the initial brunt of Mia's anger.

"I'm good but you won't be when Mia gets her hands on you," Roger informed him.

Keylan released a loud and hearty laugh. "You still at the house?"

"No. I made sure she couldn't send anyone away or anything back and I got the hell out of there. That little woman is scary."

"Yes, she can be," Keylan agreed.

"I call for another reason. The commission agreed to count your suspension game days after your doctor releases you."

"So…"

"So if you're released within the next two weeks, with the current schedule, you can be back playing before Christmas," Roger explained.

"That's great, man."

"Just doing my job as the longer you're off the court, the fewer endorsement days you get in and the less money I make."

"Some things never change with you, Roger. Talk to you tomorrow."

Keylan got in his car and made his way home. He showered and changed into jeans and a gray button-down shirt. He put on his black leather loafers and headed downstairs, where he exited through the lobby doors, only to be met by a slew of reporters. *Damn, I should've parked in the garage.*

"KJ, what's the deal with you and Mia Ramirez?" someone shouted out.

"Have you two been seeing each other long?" another woman asked.

A man yelled out, "I hear you'll be getting back in the game soon. Is that true?"

"From your ears…" Keylan replied before getting into his car and driving away. *Mia's really going to hate seeing her name in the news…again.*

It took less than twenty minutes to get to Mia's house and he smiled when he pulled his car into her driveway. He felt a huge sense of satisfaction and pride at the fact that Mia's place was no longer the dark house on the street. Keylan only hoped Mia would forgive his blatant intrusion into her life. He couldn't help himself.

He exited his car and smiled at the white lights that lined her house, the trees and shrubs. The big, colorful ornament balls that had been placed in her trees were a nice touch.

"Note to self—thank Rivers." Keylan took a deep breath, released it slowly and knocked on the door.

* * *

"Mommy, the door," Colby called out from his spot on the sofa as a knock came on the door.

"I know, son." Mia dropped the dishrag on the counter, turned off the burner under her food and walked to the door.

She opened it and the look of excitement and joy on Keylan's face eclipsed her anger. Mia's shoulders dropped and her mouth curved into a smirk. She couldn't believe how happy she was to see his overbearing self. "Hi."

"Hello, can I come in?"

Mia's hand rose and landed on her hip. "Depends." She gave him a playful scowl.

"On what?"

"Did you come bringing more Christmas surprises and gifts?"

"Just me…"

Chapter 19

Mia stepped aside and waved her hand forward. "Come in."

"Keylan," Colby called, running toward him.

Keylan bent down and picked him up. "Hey, buddy."

"Come see my tree. It plays music." He wiggled until Keylan set him down. He took his hand and Colby pulled him to his room, stopping long enough to say, "Mommy's tree don't sing."

"I know." Keylan looked over his shoulder and winked at Mia.

Mia narrowed her eyes and fought her laughter as she followed them into Colby's room, where his Charlie Brown tree had been set up. "See my tree," he said, climbing onto his bed.

Keylan noticed that not one thing had been added to the tree. It was exactly as it was when he'd bought it. "That's a really cool spot for your tree, too, right in front of your bed."

"Colby, sweetheart, play with your toys and finish the movie." She handed him the tablet that was on the dresser. "Enjoy your tree while Mommy and Keylan finish making dinner."

"Okeydoke."

Mia took Keylan's hand, led him out of the room and

back into the family room. She dropped his hand and looked around. "Nutcrackers, angels and a Santa Claus statue. Thank goodness they don't move."

"Of course it doesn't move. That would scare Colby."

"And all these gifts under this tree." She directed him to the one he'd had delivered and decorated. "Look at this thing, it's huge. I didn't think they could even get it through the door."

The corners of his mouth quirked up. "You can't have a tree or Christmas, for that matter, without gifts. It's almost as beautiful as you are." His voice was husky and his eyes dark with desire.

The way he was looking at her and the sound of his voice ignited something inside Mia. She became very warm in places that only he seemed to be able to reach. From his sexy smile and the way his eyes roamed her body, Mia felt naked in spite of the black leggings and long red T-shirt she wore.

Keylan walked up to Mia, placed both hands on her hips and lifted her as if she was a delicate doll. Mia's instincts kicked in, her legs wrapping around his waist as she circled her hands around his neck. "How much time do we have?" he asked, kissing her gently on the lips.

Mia's mind was clouded by need. "Time?" she whispered.

"Before Little Man joins us," he explained, walking them into her living room, where he sat in the bay window, where the blinds were drawn, out of the view of young eyes, with Mia straddling him.

Mia laughed. "We have about twenty minutes."

"I'll take it." Keylan buried his hands in Mia's hair and devoured her mouth.

Mia returned his kiss with a level of passion and sense of desperation she'd never felt before. As their tongues danced and Keylan's lips moved to explore her neck, he whispered how much he wanted her. The pressure that had been building between her legs demanded release. Mia's hands gripped his shoulders and she began to grind her hips against the bulge in his jeans.

Keylan placed his hands under her shirt and unclipped her bra. He cupped her breasts and squeezed her nipples as he stared up at her, matching her pelvic moves.

Mia was lost in the storm of desire. With each grind and stroke she made, the more control she seemed to lose, until something snapped. Keylan muffled the sound of her release with a mind-blowing kiss.

As Mia's movement slowed, her embarrassment grew. She buried her face in his neck and uncontrollable tears flowed. Keylan held her close and rubbed her back. "It's okay, baby."

Mia remained still for several moments. She finally built up enough courage to rise and look at him. "I… I don't know what came over me."

Keylan brushed her hair out of her face and kissed a small bead of sweat from her nose. "I hope it was me that came over you."

Mia smirked. "I'd say so. I haven't done that since high school."

"Neither have I," he assured her.

"I think I should go clean up." Mia relaxed her legs and rolled off him. "Oh, my." She looked down at the bulge in his pants.

"It's fine," he promised.

"I'm sorry," she murmured.

"I'm not." He ran the back of his hand down the side of her face. "Pleasing you pleases me. It also shows how wonderful we will be together when we do finally make love."

Mia leaned in and kissed him gently on the lips. "I'll be back in a few."

"I think I should use your guest bathroom. I need to make a few adjustments myself."

Mia covered her mouth and laughed. "Help yourself."

Mia hurried to her room and went straight to the bathroom. She turned on the shower, quickly undressed and stepped under the spray. "Mia, you've got some explaining to do," she told herself.

After washing up, Keylan collected Colby and the two of them started setting the dinner table. "Do you like the Christmas decorations? They're not scary, are they?"

Colby frowned. "No. They don't move."

Keylan nodded as he pulled out the silverware. "How about the lights outside?"

Colby's frown deepened. "They don't move, either."

Keylan laughed at the confused look on Colby's face. "How do they look?"

"They're pretty. But they don't sing."

"No, they don't." Keylan reached into the cabinet and took out three plates. He moved to the stove and raised the lids off the pots. "What do we have here?"

"Food," Colby replied.

"I can see that, son." *Son... Wow, I actually like the sound of that.*

"This looks like a roast, cabbage over here and beans and rice. Man, does your mom cook like this every Sunday?"

"Yes, she does," Mia answered, walking into the kitchen barefoot, wearing dark gray drawstring pants and a white tank top. Her wet hair was pulled back into a high ponytail. *Damn, you're beautiful.*

"What are you two up to?" Mia asked.

"We're making dinner, Mommy. I'll be right back." Colby ran from the room.

"We were making plates," he explained. "Everything looks delicious."

"Well, don't let me stop you. Please continue." Mia took a seat at the island.

"Everything for my beautiful lady?" he asked before leaning down and kissing her on the lips.

"Yes, please."

Keylan dished up three plates of food and placed them on the table.

"I'm back," Colby announced.

Mia and Keylan turned to find that Colby had changed out of his jeans and was now wearing his pajama bottoms.

"Honey, are you okay? Did you have an accident?" Mia gave him the once-over. "Why did you change clothes?"

"Mommy changed clothes. Did you have an accident?"

"That was certainly no accident," Keylan murmured.

Mia's eyes bore into Keylan's. "No, sweetheart, Mommy didn't have an accident. It was just time to change clothes."

"Let's eat and, Colby, you can tell me about the show you are watching." Keylan sat between Colby and Mia, dividing his attention between the two people that had suddenly become essential players in his life.

After dinner, Mia and Keylan cleaned up the dirty dishes before wrestling with Colby through bath time, taking his nightly asthma and allergy medicines and story time before finally getting him down for bed.

Keylan flopped onto the sofa, pulling Mia into his arms. "Is he always that energetic before it's time for bed?"

"Not usually. It's been a pretty exciting day."

Keylan took Mia's hand and brought it to his lips. "Yes, it has. How's the hand?"

"It's fine. About earlier…"

"What about it?"

Mia's cell phone rang. "Just a second." She reached for the phone and read the screen. "Hello, Auntie."

"Hi, darling. How are you?"

"I'm fine, but now's not a good time to talk."

"Oh, really, why's that?"

Mia sighed. "Keylan's here."

"Bye…"

Mia looked down at her phone and laughed.

"Everything okay?" Keylan asked.

"Yes, just my aunt checking up on me. I feel like I should explain what happened."

"I think we both know what happened and it was wonderful." He wrapped a strand of her hair around his fingers.

"I need to explain why it happened."

Keylan's forehead creased. "Why it happened?" His confusion was clear.

Mia stared at her hands. "I haven't been with a man in that way in quite some time."

Keylan used his index finger to raise her chin and stare into her eyes. "How much time?"

"Nearly five years. Not since before Colby was born."

Mia searched Keylan's face but he remained expressionless. "How's that possible? You're the most desirable woman I've ever met. I can't believe there haven't been any other men in your life."

She shrugged. "None that I've been interested in…not like that, anyway. I don't even know why I've remained on birth control all these years." Mia rose from the sofa and walked into the kitchen. "Do you want anything to drink?"

"No, I'm good."

Mia pulled out a bottle of ginger ale from the refrigerator, cracked the seal and took a drink, hoping it would calm her stomach. "Colby was born with so many health unknowns that he became my only priority. I didn't have time or the energy for much else."

"But Colby's good now."

"Yes, he is, for the most part. He still has respiratory issues from time to time." Mia sat back down and took another drink from the bottle.

Keylan's jaw tightened. "So are you saying that what happened between us was just built-up need?"

Mia could see the disappointment in his eyes and she knew she had to be very clear with her next statement. "No." She placed her bottle on the table, took his hands in hers and pushed out a deep breath. "What I'm saying is that I've never made room in my life for anyone other than my aunt, uncle and Colby. What I'm saying is that I want you to be part of my life...our life. That is, if you want that, too."

Keylan pulled Mia onto his lap. "I want that very much."

Mia cupped his face and kissed him. "Do you want to stay tonight?"

"I'd love to but I want the first time we make love to be special."

"I'm sure it will be," she whispered, hoping she didn't sound as desperate as she felt.

"I have an idea."

"What's that?" Mia was fighting hard not to show her disappointment.

"Remember when I said we should take our winter break kids on vacation to my family's private resort up on our mountain?"

"Yes."

"Why don't you let me take you this weekend? We can spend some quality alone time together and you can see for yourself what a great opportunity this could be for our kids."

Mia bit her lip and thought about all the advice her aunt

had given her over the years. She was finally ready to listen. "Well—"

Keylan held up his right hand. "Before you say no—"

"Yes."

Keylan's face lit up. "Yes… Did you just say yes?"

"Yes, I did. I know my aunt will watch Colby, so…yes."

Keylan kissed her on the corner of her mouth. "There's one thing you should know before we go any further…"

Chapter 20

Keylan didn't want to scare Mia off, but he knew if they had any chance of having something real he must be honest about who he was and what she was getting into. "You asked me about the bodyguards."

Mia nodded but remained silent.

"Do you remember what my family, specifically my brother, went through with the EPA a few months ago?"

"Yeah." Mia frowned. "They claimed that your company, under your brother's leadership, disposed of something illegal."

"Gas cylinders, which are not only illegal, they're also bad for the environment. The EPA claimed it was done all for money."

"That's crazy, since your family's worth millions."

"It's more like billions," he corrected.

"Seriously?" Mia's face contorted.

"Seriously."

"Well, the real story came out, right? People lied."

"You're right, but what's not wildly known is that one of our biggest competitors was behind the whole setup. They even tried to go after my brother but got China by mistake."

Mia's brows drew together. "What do you mean, they got China by mistake?"

"She was driven off the road while driving Alexander's car. She ended up hitting a tree."

"My God."

"Which is why my family has increased everyone's security." He held her gaze, trying to keep his emotions under control because the thought of someone coming after him but getting Mia and Colby by mistake made his blood run cold. "That security includes anyone in our lives, too."

"Are you saying we could be in danger?"

Keylan watched as Mia's eyes darted to the area of the house where her son slept. "No. The men who were driving the car were eventually caught but they're refusing to name who hired them."

"That's good. I mean, it's good that they got caught, not that they won't talk," Mia explained.

"I know what you meant. We don't think there's anything looming against us from that threat, but we can't be certain and we're a very wealthy family, so we always have to be careful. Now, with the IRS and OSHA in the mix, we're being extra cautions. Which is why I've assigned a security detail to watch over you and Colby."

"You've done what?" Her eyebrows stood at attention.

"When you're with the Kingsleys, you're with the Kingsleys. We won't take a chance with your safety, even if it's not really necessary. I hope you're okay with that." Keylan was praying that she would be.

"I'm okay that you care enough to want to protect us, but I'm not sure how I feel about being under constant observation."

"I get that, but as long as we're together you will be, and not just from my security."

Mia released an audible breath. "The media."

"Yes. My security team will be discreet. The media

won't be, especially when we're together. Can you handle that?"

Mia rose from his lap and walked over to stand in front of the massive Christmas tree that now graced her family room. Her back was turned to him and her arms were folded across her waist.

Keylan knew things could be over before they'd even gotten started and the thought was killing him. He was only waiting for the words so he could figure out how to counter her argument and convince her to change her mind. He wasn't prepared to lose them.

Mia turned to face him and his eyes held hers. Keylan could almost see the different ideas and scenarios as they crossed her mind.

It was several long and painful moments before Mia finally whispered, "I can handle it."

Keylan smiled and stood. He wrapped his arms around her waist and held her close to his heart. The idea of losing her scared him beyond anything he'd experienced before. He whispered, "Everything's going to be fine. I promise."

"I know," she said.

"One more thing." Keylan released her, pulled out his wallet and retrieved two business cards. "Here you go."

Mia accepted both cards. "'Her Winter Wear,'" Mia read from one card. "Who's Kirby?" She held up the second card.

"Her Winter Wear is a store down from the Galleria. You'll need to go by there for your outfits for our trip." Mia shook her head. "Yes. You have no idea how cold it'll be on our mountain. I'm talking below-zero weather. Baby, let me do this for you, please."

"It doesn't look like I have much of a choice. It won't be a very romantic trip if I'm trembling and my teeth are chattering the whole time."

"Oh, you'll be trembling, and your teeth just might chatter—but not from the cold," he promised, gifting her with a wicked grin.

Mia licked her lips and gave him a shy smile. "Do I ask for Kirby?" She glanced again at the second card.

"Only if you need help with your security." Keylan laughed.

"What?"

"Kirby is heading up your security detail, making sure everything runs smoothly."

"Everything like what?"

Keylan removed his phone from his pocket and sent a text. "I'm going to let Kirby explain."

There was a knock on the door and Keylan smiled. He walked to the door and opened it. "Come in. It's time you met Mia."

Mia's mouth fell open and closed quickly. She offered the beautiful petite brown-skinned woman standing before her, wearing jeans and a hot-pink blouse and looking like she belonged on the cover of a fashion magazine, a lopsided grin.

Keylan smirked. "Not what you expected?"

"Not at all," she said, offering her hand. "Pleased to meet you."

"Likewise," Kirby replied, clearly not surprised by Mia's reaction.

"We thought it would be more appropriate if you had someone less obvious but just as deadly protecting you and Colby," Keylan explained.

"I assure you, ma'am, I'm quite capable of protecting you and your son. I'm a martial arts expert and I can take down anyone that gets in my way, regardless of their size."

"I have no doubt. And call me Mia. Please have a seat."

"Thank you."

"Why don't you explain the home surveillance—?"

"Surveillance?"

Keylan took Mia's hand in his. "You didn't think those ornamental balls in the tree were just for decoration, did you?"

"Um, yeah."

Kirby pulled out a small tablet, pressed a couple of screens and views of multiple angles of the outside of Mia's house appeared.

"What the...?"

"I can monitor what's happening outside and around your house and the street, for that matter, regardless of where I may be," Kirby assured her.

"Is that really necessary?" Mia's eyes jumped from Kirby to Keylan.

"This is more about the press," Keylan said.

"The press?" Mia declared.

"They tend to sneak around looking for opportunities for stories. Some even try to go through your trash when it's left out on the curb overnight," Keylan warned.

Mia pulled her hand free and walked into the kitchen. Keylan followed her. "I know it seems like a lot to deal with—"

"Because it is." Mia looked up at him. "But I can handle it."

Keylan leaned down and kissed her gently on the lips. His phone rang and after checking the screen he said, "Baby, I have to take this."

"No problem."

"Kirby, can you go over the rest of the details for Mia's security with her?"

Mia's eyes grew wide. "The rest..."

Keylan walked outside and brought the phone to his ear. "What's up, Roger?"

"It's done. You're back in."

"Really?" he asked, surprised.

"You doubted me?"

"No, but I didn't think you'd know anything that fast." Fear marred his excitement.

"The doctors cleared you and you've already met the community service hours with working at the foundation full-time, so you're good."

"That's great."

"You don't sound like it's great," Roger concluded. "You lace up tomorrow night. They're expecting you at the ten-o'clock news conference before the two-hour practice. You fly out right after tomorrow night's game. You can't play yet, but you are expected to be on the sidelines. You'll miss tomorrow's, Wednesday's and Thursday's games, but after that you hit the floor."

Keylan really was happy to be getting back to work, but his relationship with Mia was so new…fragile. He wasn't sure how well she could handle what was about to happen. "I have to prepare Mia."

"Prepare Mia for what? You're an NBA superstar, not to mention a bona fide billionaire. She has to know what that means. Groupies—"

"This isn't about women. It's about her privacy and our time together," he replied.

"Look, man, we've talked about this already. Settling down at the height of your career is a bad idea. Don't get me wrong—I liked Mia and I think her kid is great. I just don't think now's the time to be playing husband and father to someone else's four-year-old son."

"I'm so glad you didn't make a derogatory comment about Colby, because I would have had to fire you on the spot."

"You know me better than that."

"I do… Sorry. I'm not playing at anything. I'm in love with Mia and Colby." Keylan was done fighting his feelings and he was prepared to do whatever was necessary to prove that to both of them.

Roger sighed. "Okay. I got your back no matter what."

"Thanks. Now let's hope Mia does, too."

Keylan walked back into the house just as Kirby and Mia wrapped up their conversation. "If you have any more questions or if you need anything, call me or just press the panic button I gave you."

"I will, and thanks for making those adjustments we discussed."

"What adjustments?" Keylan asked, his tone harsher than he intended.

"You can go, Kirby. I'll explain things to Keylan."

Kirby's eyes danced between Keylan and Mia. Clearly she was looking for permission to leave.

Keylan nodded and Kirby hurried away.

"Wow, you really are the boss."

"What's that supposed to mean?"

Mia shrugged, took a seat and crossed her legs. "It's just every time I suggested an alternative to her plan, she reminded me that you were her boss. Of course, I reminded her that me and my son were the people she was protecting and if she wanted my cooperation she had to be flexible."

"What adjustments do you think need to be made?"

"If we're going to make this work—"

"If…"

"Yes, *if.* I can't have my life changed completely."

Keylan understood that this was all new to Mia and her wanting to maintain some form of normalcy in her life was completely understandable. However, his first concern was for their safety. He went and sat next to her on the sofa.

"I get our being together will be an adjustment, one I'm willing to make. But I need to set some boundaries."

"Like what?"

"Like, I don't need to be driven around from place to place. I'm more than capable of driving myself. Your security can follow us around if they must, but that's non-negotiable."

"What else?" Keylan folded his arms.

"They can watch from a distance. We don't need a shadow. It's bad enough having my house and place of work under constant surveillance."

"Wait—"

"No, you wait. If they sense something is wrong, they can absolutely make their presence known. I just don't need anyone following us around in the grocery store."

Keylan's face went blank. "Anything else?"

"Nope, that's it." Mia slid over, climbed onto Keylan's lap and used her right index finger to smooth his wrinkled forehead. "Stop brooding and kiss me."

Keylan captured her finger and kissed it. "You're going to make me crazy."

"I know." Mia imprisoned his face in the palms of her hands, kissing him passionately on the lips and losing herself in the moment. "You sure you can't stay tonight?"

"I wish I could. I have news," he whispered.

"News?"

"Yes. I'm going back to work."

Mia went poker-faced. "What…? When?"

"Tomorrow."

Chapter 21

Mia fought the tears she wanted to shed. She knew she was being extremely ridiculous but she couldn't help it. She enjoyed working with Keylan every day and she was looking forward to the plans they had just made. *Don't be that girl.* Mia pasted on a fake smile and said, "That's great news. When do you leave?"

"In the morning, and I have you to thank, too. If you hadn't submitted all my volunteer hours so diligently, Roger would have never been able to pull this off so quickly."

Yeah, well, that was before. "You're welcome. I was just doing my job." Mia was choking on disappointment and shame for even feeling such a way. *Don't say it... Don't say it.* She lowered her head but before she knew it, the words were falling out of her mouth. "I guess we have to postpone our weekend."

Keylan used his thumb and index finger of his right hand and captured her chin. He raised her head and held her gaze. "Of course not, baby. This week's games are tomorrow, Wednesday and Thursday. I have practice Friday morning and I'm off Saturday and Sunday. We can leave Friday night and return Sunday night, just as planned."

"Really?" Mia's face lit up and he laughed.

"Yes, sweetheart, really." Keylan sealed his promise with a mind-blowing kiss. "It's getting late. I better go."

"If you must," she teased.

"I know I won't be playing, but I'll be on the sidelines. Will you and Colby watch?"

The look of excitement in Keylan's eyes at such a simple request made Mia's heart skip several beats. "Of course we will."

"Walk me out." They stood in her doorway and Keylan gave her one final kiss before saying, "Don't forget to bring something not-so-warm and preferably see-through for our nights in front of the fireplace."

Mia was suddenly warm herself as she stood and watched Keylan get into his car and drive off.

"Thanks for coming with me, Sandra. I'm not sure I could have done all this without you," Mia declared the next day.

"Spending the afternoon shopping with other people's money? Color me in." Sandra laughed. "I still can't believe this change. Usually you send me with a list and your credit card to get gifts for you. You even had me get my own gift card. Now, not only have you bought your own Christmas gifts for everyone, you got me helping you pick out clothes for your sexy weekend with KJ."

"Shh…" Mia looked around the store.

"No one's paying attention to us. The only thing those personal shoppers—" Sandra pointed to the two saleswomen pouring wine into glasses and arranging an assortment of finger foods onto platters "—are concerned with is making sure you're happy and willing to spend as much of KJ's money as possible. I wonder what kind of credit line he has here, anyway."

"It doesn't matter. I'm not looking to spend—"

"Here we are," the taller of the two women began as she handed them both a glass of wine. "We have a few refreshments, too. Please enjoy." She pointed to the plates the smaller woman had placed on the table that sat between them.

"Thank you. You really didn't have to go to so much trouble," Mia told her.

"It's no problem at all. I'll be right back with a few outfits for you to consider." She disappeared behind a black curtain.

"Girl, this is good." Sandra took another sip of her wine. "I'm glad we waited to go shopping in the afternoon and made this our last stop, because I'm going to need a few more glasses of this. Where's Colby?"

"He's with my uncle. It's their day for male bonding."

"Cool. What all are you getting here?" Sandra glanced around the room. "I've never been to a store where there are no racks or clothes, just a few well-dressed mannequins and books."

Mia followed Sandra's line of sight, taking in the store's contemporary gray-and-white furnishings, the expensive paintings and Oriental rugs that covered the slate flooring. "Me, either, but Keylan asked me to come here. It's certainly not what I expected."

"Rich people." Both women laughed and nodded.

"Here we are," the saleswoman announced, rolling in a rack of outfits. "There are several things here for you to choose from. I'm sure I got the size right, but if not, we can take care of it."

"Nice," Sandra replied.

"Mr. Kingsley would like for you to select at least three complete snow suits, boots and a coat."

"Girl…" Sandra started, checking out the food.

Mia rose and walked over to the rack to take a closer

look at the outfits. "Oh, wow, these are all very nice. They feel warm, too."

"They are, so you'll be very comfortable in the harsh winter weather," the saleswoman assured her.

Mia nodded.

Sandra joined her at the clothes rack. "This one is too cute." Sandra pulled out a red snowsuit.

"Excuse me for one moment." The saleslady went to help the other customer in the store.

I can't believe I'm doing this.

"What's wrong?" Sandra placed the snowsuit against her body as she stood in front of a trio of mirrors.

Mia's shoulders dropped. "I don't think I can do this."

"Do what?"

"This…all of this." Mia flopped back down in her chair. "I'm not the type of woman who lets a man, a rich man at that, buy her clothes."

Sandra turned to face her. "I don't know why the hell not. That man is crazy about you. So what if he wants to spend a little cash on you?"

"You don't think it makes me seem like I'm…I don't know. Like some gold digger?"

"No, it doesn't, because you're not. You're a twenty-six-year-old single mother who works hard and deserves to have a guy like KJ who wants to do nice things for you. If I was you, I'd sit back and enjoy it." She winked at her friend.

"Thanks, Sandra."

"Anytime. Now, I'm going to go try this on. In case you want to get me something else for Christmas."

"Girl, please, these clothes don't even have prices on them."

"One can always dream." Sandra stepped into the dressing room.

A tall, fair-skinned woman wearing a black and white

Chanel suit, a pair of matching Chanel heels and a cluster of pearls around her neck took the seat next to Mia. "Your friend's right, you know."

"Excuse me?"

"I couldn't help but overhear your conversation. If your man wants to buy you clothes, you should let him. After all—" she sat back in the chair and crossed her legs "—he is a Kingsley and can most certainly afford it."

Mia turned in her chair to face the stranger. *Who the hell is this woman?* "Do I know you?"

"No, but I know you, Mia Ramirez." Mia gave the woman the once-over as she reached for her purse, contemplating if she should use her panic button. "No need to call for your security, my dear."

"Who are you?" Mia frowned.

"Just someone who's been where you are and thought I'd offer some friendly advice. My name is Lisa Barrington."

Mia's expression dulled. "I see. So, what, you once dated Keylan or something?"

"Heavens, no." She laughed and raised her left hand, flashing what had to be an at-least ten-carat diamond ring. "He was an unwanted guest at my wedding last year."

Mia's brow puckered. "What?"

"Keylan plays on the team with my husband, Clay. Just before we got married, he told Clay that they were too young to be tied down and that he should run while he still had the chance."

"Oh. I'm sorry." Mia wasn't sure how she felt about this woman's assertion about Keylan's thoughts on marriage.

Lisa laughed. "Don't be. Clay was too smart to listen to KJ. Besides, he was drunk at the time and he has since apologized. He's been a good friend of ours for years. Now let's see if you're smart enough to listen to me."

Mia felt a sudden sense of relief to hear Keylan's revised

feelings about marriage, even though they were a long way away from even the idea of such a commitment. "Okay, I'm listening." Mia folded her arms across her chest.

"Keylan's a good guy, and when he first joined the league he had a lot to prove."

"What do you mean?" Her curiosity was piqued.

"Well—"

"What do you think, Mia?" Sandra called as she entered the room. "Oh, sorry."

"Sandra, this is—"

"Clay Barrington's wife." Awe transformed Sandra's face.

"Lisa. Her name is Lisa," Mia amended, shaking her head. She still couldn't believe how much Sandra knew about basketball and all the players.

"Pleased to meet you," Lisa said, offering her hand.

"Nice to meet you, too." Sandra shook her hand before she reached for the bottle of wine. "Care for some?" She poured herself another glass.

"I'd love some, thank you. That outfit looks great on you, by the way," Lisa noted.

"Thank you." Savoring the compliment, Sandra filled another glass and handed it to her. "Mia, you want more?"

"No, I'm fine. Can you give us a few minutes?"

"Oh, sure, I'll just go change."

Mia waited for Sandra to leave before asking, "What did you mean when you said Keylan had a lot to prove?"

"It didn't matter how good his stats were, how high or which round he came out in the draft. He was a privileged billionaire's son. He had to prove himself on the floor, which he did." Lisa took a drink from her glass. "Personally, I think he took on that playboy and bad boy persona to fit in and just ran with it."

"I can understand that." Mia nodded.

"So when I see him standing up for you, claiming you, wanting to take care of you, it tells me that this is real."

Mia smiled. "I hope so."

"Ignore any rumors and don't worry about the groupies. Keylan is an honorable man, just like my Clay. Just be careful of the media. They can be brutal." Lisa checked her watch. "I should go."

Both women stood. "Thank you. I appreciate the advice," Mia remarked.

"Anytime." Lisa pulled out a business card and handed it to Mia. "Call me so we can all have dinner."

"Will do."

Lisa collected her packages and walked out of the store.

Mia sat and let Lisa's words take root. She was determined to make things work with Keylan. He had her heart and she was more than ready to give him the rest of her, too.

"What'd I miss?" Sandra asked, hanging the snowsuit back on the rack.

"Not much." Mia pulled out her phone. "Can you get the saleslady? I finally know what I want."

Chapter 22

The week had moved at a snail's pace for Mia. She was counting down the days until the weekend, when she'd finally be alone with the man she loved. Keylan had returned to his life before he'd met her and Colby, and Mia was determined to not let his absence cripple her by keeping busy. She found herself watching the clock each day, willing the hours to pass. Her daily video conference calls with Keylan were the only thing that got her through the long nights, although after she'd hung up and gone to bed, she usually woke wrapped in moist sheets after Keylan paid her a visit in her dreams. They had found ways to deal with the distance together.

Keylan taught Mia how to use her imagination, hands and the sound of his voice to combat the lonely nights apart. Mia had never considered doing such things, especially with her partner watching from a video screen. Keylan, on the other hand, had no reservation with showing Mia how much he missed and needed her. The fact that they shared such intimate moments only heightened the anticipation for when they would finally be together.

Those moments, not to mention the thoughtful daily gifts he sent her and her son, took the sting out of his absence. With the exception of the flowers, everything Keylan sent

Colby was practical: additional shoes that matched his own and a video system with games loaded that catered to his age and specific needs. By far, her favorite thing he would do was acknowledge her and Colby during interviews or whenever the camera was on him. Keylan developed a secret message for them. He would tap two fingers against his heart, signaling how much he cared for them and that they were always with him. The weekend couldn't get there fast enough for either of them.

Friday had finally arrived and Mia sat quietly flipping through a magazine in the VIP lounge for private plane boarding in Houston Hobby Airport. She was trying to keep her excitement in check but she was losing that battle. She kept imagining all the wicked things Keylan had promised over the past week that they would do; she was finding it hard to sit still. She couldn't believe how all right she felt about leaving Colby for two whole days. Yes, she had left him with her aunt and uncle many times, but usually for no longer than a day and even then, she'd felt bad. Fortunately, Colby never felt that way; he loved the independence it gave him. Mia, on the other hand, wasn't sure how she felt about that, either.

Mia heard her name being called and was surprised to see where that sound came from. "Kirby, what are you doing here? You going somewhere?" She noticed the small roller bag Kirby held with one hand and the rather large phone she had to her ear.

Kirby stopped in front of her and smiled. "Yes, sir. She's right here." Kirby handed Mia the type of device she'd only seen in movies: a satellite phone.

"Hello…?"

"Hi, baby." Keylan released an audible breath.

"Keylan." Mia's mouth curved into a wide smile and Kirby stepped away from her.

"I've been trying to reach you."

Mia could hear the worry in his voice. "Sorry, my phone died and my charger is in my checked bag."

"I guess that explains it."

"Where are you?"

"I'm stuck in Atlanta a bit longer. We have some NBA promotional work and a few more interviews I have to do before I can leave."

"Oh." Mia's smile slipped. "I understand."

"Stop, don't do that. The only thing that's changed is that I'm going to have to meet you there and I won't get to see the look on your face when you find out where you're going," Keylan explained.

"What?"

"Kirby's going to fly out with you and I'll meet you at the resort this evening."

"Are you sure we just shouldn't postpone things?"

"Absolutely not!" His voice was firm, which only excited Mia more. "We need this weekend, baby. I need you."

"I need you, too," she whispered.

"Good. They will get you there and settled. I'll be by your side before you know it, I promise."

They. "Okay."

"See you soon, my love," Keylan said before ending the call.

Mia loved it when Keylan called her that, although he had never told her he loved her. She had yet to say the words to him, either, but she planned to this weekend. Mia was done holding back.

"Here you go." Mia tried to hand Kirby back the phone.

"No, that's for you," Kirby insisted.

"I don't need this thing. My charger is in my bag. I'll charge my phone when I get to the resort. By the way, where is this resort?"

Kirby frowned. "Mr. Kingsley didn't tell you?"

"It was going to be a surprise," she murmured, pushing down her disappointment.

"It's in Aspen. Actually, it's above Aspen...in the mountains," Kirby revealed, and Mia could see how much she hated spoiling the surprise.

"Really, have you been there before?"

"Yes, the Kingsleys have had many retreats and events there for their family and staff," Kirby answered.

"Tell me about it." Curiosity was getting the best of Mia.

"It would be better if you see it for yourself. I really don't want to spoil that moment for you, too. You ready to go?"

"As I'll ever be."

Kirby simpered at the tall, handsome man she waved forward. "Mia Ramirez, this is Neil, my husband."

Mia offered her hand. "Pleased to meet you."

"Likewise." He gave her hand a small shake.

"He'll be joining us."

"Great. So will you two be spending the weekend at the resort, too?" Mia wasn't sure how she felt about all these new developments but at this point all she wanted was to see Keylan.

"No, ma'am," Neil quickly volunteered.

He grinned and Kirby blushed. "Neil just got back from a six-month deployment. He's a Navy SEAL."

"Oh...I see." Mia hoped her face wasn't as red as the nail polish she wore. She knew exactly why he'd answered so quickly and she completely understood. "Thank you for your service."

Neil nodded. "After we get you settled, we'll be staying at a lodge in the city. No worries, the resort has its own security in place."

"I'm not worried." At least she wasn't until she walked out the door and saw the jet that was awaiting their arrival.

"You not afraid to fly, are you?" Kirby lifted her left eyebrow.

"Not in an adult plane."

Kirby laughed. "This is an adult plane." She grabbed Mia's hand and pulled her forward. "This is a Gulfstream IV-SP, and it's one of the safest and coolest planes out there."

Mia climbed the stairs and entered an atmosphere of elegance and pure indulgence. "Oh, my goodness." She couldn't help but marvel at what looked like someone's expensive and eloquently decorated living room. Beautiful wood-grain surfaces were offset by plush, cream leather sofas and reclining chairs, all disguised as an airplane.

"I know. There's even a master suite in the back if you prefer to sleep through the trip."

"No, thank you." Mia smiled as she replayed Keylan's voice promising to make her a part of the mile-high club.

"Take a seat. I'll go inform the crew that we're ready." Kirby handed her things to her husband before turning to leave.

Mia sat in a chair across from Neil. "A Navy SEAL and your wife's a security expert. Your house must be the safest one in your neighborhood," she joked.

Neil smiled. "It would be if we had a home."

Mia scowled. "What?"

"People like us with careers that require so much time, commitment and travel aren't exactly the settling-down-and-staying-in-one-place types. The best part about our relationship is that we understand and accept that about each other. We can hardly keep a plant alive. We own a nice condo downtown that we rarely see."

"That's too bad." Mia felt a sadness that she didn't want to examine.

"What's too bad?" Kirby asked, taking a seat next to her husband.

"The fact we can't keep a plant alive," Neil proclaimed.

Kirby shrugged. "That's why we have silk plants. Buckle up."

Mia sat back as the jet raced down the runway. She couldn't help but wonder if the unsolicited words of experience being sent her way were some type of warning.

Keylan handed his phone to Roger. "Let's get this over with."

"Mia cool?"

"Yeah, but I know she's disappointed." Keylan moved to stand in front of a green screen. "She was expecting us to travel together."

"She might as well get used to it," Roger reminded, keeping his eyes on his cell phone.

No, she shouldn't. Keylan stood stone-faced as a photographer took all the pictures he needed. He was thankful that this was a shoot that required a serious look; otherwise he wouldn't have made it through. All he could think about was the disappointment he'd heard in Mia's voice, and the idea he caused that was making him crazy. He was so lost in his thoughts and regrets that he hadn't heard the photographer say they were done.

"KJ, you all right?"

"I'm good. Are we done?"

"Yes, but the executives would like to take you out to dinner to celebrate wrapping this campaign and the start of the next one."

"Can't." Keylan walked into the trailer and started removing the gray suit he'd just been photographed wearing.

"What do you mean, you can't? These folks just offered you a new multimillion-dollar advertising deal." Roger put his phone away.

"A deal that I haven't signed yet," he reminded Roger.

"Dude, what's wrong with you?"

"There's nothing wrong with me. I have a plane to catch." Keylan quickly changed out of the suit and into a pair of jeans, a white button-down shirt and a leather jacket.

"A plane that you own. Come on, man, this is business."

"That's a dinner that can wait. I've already pushed Mia back for business once, which was a mistake, and it won't happen again." His tone was firm and final.

"What do you mean, a mistake? Business always comes before pleasure, KJ." Roger's nose crinkled.

Keylan glared at Roger. "Mia is more than just pleasure. I thought you got that." He sat and put on his sneakers.

"I guess I didn't realize how serious you are about your feelings for her."

Keylan stood. "Then let me be perfectly clear. Mia and Colby are my future. Got it?" Keylan snapped.

"Got it!"

"Good, now call for the car. I'm headed to the airport." Keylan exited the trailer.

Chapter 23

Mia stood in the grand foyer of what had to be the biggest and most beautiful house she'd ever seen. Between the huge, wood double doors that opened to white-marble floors that looked like snow and the hundred feet you had to walk just to reach the middle of the entrance hall, Mia knew she wasn't in Texas anymore. She was still reeling from the airplane and helicopter rides up the side of the mountain, so she wasn't convinced that any of this was real.

"Are you telling me this is someone's house? I thought we were coming to a resort."

The corners of Kirby's mouth flew up. "Did you not see the sign when we pulled up into the driveway?"

"You mean that parking lot? No, I missed the sign."

"It read 'The Resort.' That's what the Kingsleys named this house," Kirby informed her.

"Again…" Mia took a step forward and turned in a slow circle. She eyed two large living areas to her left, a grand dining room that easily seated thirty people to the right, and a double marble staircase with so much more house behind it. "This is actually someone's house?"

"It most certainly is, miss," a voice answered from behind her.

She turned toward the sound. "Mia Ramirez, this is Mr. and Mrs. Phillip. They look after the estate for the Kingsleys."

"Welcome to 'The Resort,'" the older, dark-skinned, gray-haired gentleman, wearing black pants and a white shirt, greeted her. "This beautiful young woman is my wife." He pointed to the lovely, fair-skinned, gray-haired lady, wearing a black dress with a white apron, standing by his side.

"Hush up." She swatted at his hand. "My name is Alice, and my husband is Emile."

"It's very nice to meet you both," Mia replied.

"Come in and warm up. Emile, get the child's bags," she ordered.

"I'll help you with that, sir," Neil offered.

"I got it," Emile insisted, reaching for Mia's white Louis Vuitton luggage, another one of Keylan's practical gifts.

"Let me get you something warm to drink," Alice offered, glancing at all her guests. "We have all types of coffee, tea and cocoa, or if you'd like something stronger, I can help you with that, too."

"Cocoa would be great," Mia replied.

Neil nudged Kirby. "Thank you, but we're going to head down the mountain before the snow starts getting too bad." Kirby turned her attention to Mia. "As promised, the security here is second to none and Keylan trusts them completely, but if you'd like us to stay we can."

Mia could see how anxious Neil was to get his wife alone and she could relate one hundred percent. "That won't be necessary—you two should go. I'll be fine."

"Are you sure?" Kirby asked.

"She's sure," Neil insisted.

"I'm good." Mia chuckled as she pushed Kirby toward the door. "Now go enjoy yourselves."

"You, too." Kirby winked at Mia.

That's the plan.

"How about you go relax in the family room and I'll bring you that cocoa?"

"Thank you, Ms. Alice." Mia stood in silence for several moments, as she wasn't exactly sure where that was.

"It's the room directly across from the staircase," Ms. Alice directed.

"Thank you." Mia walked into the family room and her breath caught at the magnificent sight before her. The fifty-foot, glass-and-wood vaulted ceiling with a view of snowcapped mountains was breathtaking and clearly the room's focal point. It was only second to the beauty of the stone fireplace on the left wall, which was flanked by glass windows, offering a view of an iced-over lake. The expensive paintings, rugs, leather and glass furnishings were mere understudies to the room's two superstars. The image reminded Mia of something she'd see in an architectural magazine.

"Wow…"

"It's something else, isn't it?" Alice asked as she entered the room.

"Yes, ma'am, it most certainly is."

"These rooms have been the subject of many magazines over the years," she informed her, smiling.

"I bet."

"Here you go." Alice handed Mia her cocoa. "I hope you like whipped cream. It's fresh."

Mia accepted the large mug and napkin. "I sure do. Thank you." She took a sip. "Delicious."

"KJ should be here before dinner but if you'd like to eat now, I can make you a little something."

"No, this is great. Can I ask you a question?"

"Of course."

"How big is this house?" Mia's eyebrows stood at attention.

"Let's sit." Alice directed Mia over to one of the two sofas in front of the fireplace. "This is the main house and it's about ten thousand square feet. The east wing is about another five thousand and the west wing is close to eight thousand. They added the gym on that side of the house."

Mia knew her eyes were about as wide as her mug. "All this for one family."

Alice laughed. "Ms. Victoria and Ms. Elizabeth were raising five rambunctious boys. They needed the space. Then there was little Kristen, who was always trying to prove she was just as tough and could keep up with her brother and cousins, too."

"How long have you worked for the family?"

"Nearly thirty years. They're our extended family. The Kingsleys have helped us raised three sons, all of whom have gone to work for the Kingsleys in some capacity."

Mia took another drink from her mug. "This still seems like a lot of house for one family."

"The east and west wings were added much later, when they decided to lease the house out when they weren't using it."

"Oh..."

"I'll save the grand tour for KJ, but let me show you to your room. You've had a long trip. I'm sure you could use some rest."

Mia followed Alice up what seemed like an endless amount of steps and down a quiet hall that showcased photos of the Kingsley family in all stages of development. Leading the way, Alice stopped in front of a set of double doors. "KJ insisted that you be put in this room." She opened the door and stepped aside.

Mia crossed the threshold and stopped. "Oh, my..."

"Beautiful, isn't it?"

Mia nodded slowly. She had no words for the beauty of nature she was viewing through another wall of windows. "More mountains, a river and is that a...waterfall?"

"You're not just seeing this, sweetie." Alice reassured her, walking into the room. "All the rooms have beautiful views but this one is my favorite. Would you like me to help you unpack your luggage?"

"That won't be necessary, but—" Mia looked around the sparsely decorated room "—where are they and where's all the furniture?"

Alice must've noticed Mia's confused look because she started to explain. "Keylan never liked a lot of furniture, which is why there's just the big bed, nightstands and that long chaise. His mother insisted on that wall TV." She pointed to the space above the fireplace.

Mia looked at the framed picture hanging in the spot Alice pointed to. "What TV?"

"That photo is actually a TV. The remote is in the nightstand. This way to the dressing and bathrooms."

"Bathrooms?"

"Yes." They walked to the left side of the room to where there were two doors. The first led to a large, circular, walk-in closet. There was a wood island in the middle of the space with dark wood and glass cabinets, half of which were filled with men's clothes.

"Did Keylan have his things sent ahead?"

"Heavens, no, he keeps some clothes here."

"Of course he does." Mia spotted her luggage, which had been placed on a wide bench.

"Let me show you the bathroom."

Mia followed her out of the dressing room and into the bathroom. She couldn't believe how big the two-headed shower and the Jacuzzi bathtub were. "Those two doors are the water closets."

"He has two toilets?"

"Ms. Victoria insisted that they all have two."

Mia laughed. "I'm sure she had her reasons."

"I'll let you get settled. And just so you know, you're the only woman Keylan has ever brought here."

Mia smiled. "Thank you."

Mia returned to the closet, opened her suitcase and found her phone charger. She removed the phone from her purse and connected it, then pulled out the satellite phone Kirby had given her and dialed her aunt.

"It's about time you called," Mavis scolded, answering on the first ring.

"How did you know it was me? I'm not calling from my phone."

"Keylan called and gave us the number, as well as the one to the house."

"He did?" Mia felt giddy at the idea that Keylan enjoyed looking out for her and Colby.

"Yes, he did, and you had thirty more minutes before I was about to call you."

"I'm sorry. This place is just so amazing. I was distracted."

"Well, take pictures," she ordered when Mia heard her son in the background. "Here's Colby."

"Hi, Mommy."

"Hi, little man. How are you?"

"I'm good. You good?"

Mia looked around the room and smiled. "I'm good, too. I love you."

"Love you, Mommy. Bye." Mia heard the phone drop.

"Off he goes," her aunt said, sniggering.

"I'm surprised he didn't ask for Keylan."

"He didn't have to. Keylan talked to him a few minutes ago."

"Really?" Mia couldn't hide her surprise or delight.

"Yep, and if I didn't know who his deadbeat dad was, I'd swear Colby was Keylan's."

Mia decided to ignore her aunt's comment; she wasn't about to take the bait. "Sounds like everything's under control."

"As always. Now you just relax and have a good time. I love you."

"Love you, too." Mia disconnected the call and placed the phone on the nightstand. "Okay, let's go relax." She grabbed her bag of toiletries and headed to the bathroom. She undressed and jumped into the shower. With the warm water and the different body sprays pounding her body, she couldn't help but relax. After the longest shower she'd had in a while, she wrapped her body in the thickest and plushest towel she'd ever felt.

Mia walked back into the bedroom to find that a tray had been placed next to the bed with a plate of four steak sliders, fruit and a canister of hot cocoa. Mia took a bite of one sandwich and, before she knew it, she had cleaned the plate. She poured herself a cup of cocoa and sat on the bed. Knowing that she had a few hours before Keylan would arrive, she decided to forgo dressing and just lay back on the bed to enjoy the view.

Mia had no idea how much time had passed when she rolled onto her back, moaned and refused to open her eyes. She knew she was having the same dream she'd been having for the last week and didn't want it to end. Mia could feel the warmth of Keylan's breath on her face. She could smell his cologne and feel his lips and nose slide down and across her breasts. "Oh, baby, please don't stop."

* * *

Keylan couldn't believe the depth of his joy when he walked into his bedroom and found Mia lying across his bed wrapped in a towel. The light from the moon, reflecting off the icy river and pouring in the room, was like a small spotlight showing him what was now his.

Traveling the short distance from the door to his bed was more like walking a ten-mile stretch with weights on his feet. He stood next to the bed and just gazed down at Mia's sleeping form. As he stood there and undressed, his heart and body grew in anticipation. The day certainly hadn't gone as planned. From agreeing to do an impromptu photo shoot after his required NBA promotional responsibilities— a mistake he wouldn't make again—to the weather delays at the airport, he had just known their night was ruined. Oh, how wrong he was.

He removed a condom from his nightstand and rolled it on before joining Mia on the bed. He lay next to Mia and kissed her gently on the lips.

Keylan thought the satisfied smile that appeared meant she'd woken up. When she remained still, he ran his nose and tongue across her partially exposed chest. He kissed his way down the valley of her breasts and when Mia urged him not to stop, he could no longer hold back.

"I won't, baby," he whispered.

Mia's eyes popped open. "You're really here. I'm not dreaming."

"No, my love, and both our dreams are about to come true."

Chapter 24

Keylan pulled the towel from Mia's body and rolled on top of her. "I missed you like crazy, baby."

Mia cupped his face with her palm. "Show me," she demanded, reaching for him with her other hand, placing it at her entrance. "I know it's been a while, but I'm not made of glass and I won't break."

It was like a pair of invisible handcuffs had been removed with the words she spoke. Keylan thrust his hips forward and Mia's legs flew around his waist. As the walls of her body began to engulf him with each inch she took, Keylan began making sounds that even he didn't recognize until he was buried deep inside her.

He managed to calm himself long enough to gaze into her lust-filled eyes and whisper, "I'm in love with you, Mia."

"And I love you."

With those words piercing his heart, Keylan lost himself in her, confessing his love and promising her a future together as he left his mark all over her body.

After nearly an hour of treating Mia's body like his favorite meal he couldn't get enough of, and only after she'd reached satisfaction multiple times, did Keylan allow himself to enjoy his own release…loudly.

They both lay flat on their backs, sweating and breathing hard. "Wow, that was way better than my dreams."

"I know," Keylan agreed.

Mia rolled to her side and faced Keylan. She propped up her head with her right hand. "So, about the things you said."

Keylan turned his head toward her. "You can't help it, can you?"

"What do you mean?"

"You're overthinking this. I meant every word I said." He rolled onto his side and faced her. "I'm in love with you. The three of us have a bright future ahead of us."

Mia pushed him onto his back and climbed on top of him. "Okay, smarty-pants. Since you seem to know what I'm thinking—" she swerved her hips against his, groaning "—what do I want now?"

Keylan raised his head and watched as Mia kissed her way down his smooth, sweaty chest past his stomach to his crotch. "Baby…" was all he could get out before Mia gripped the base of his shaft with her right hand and guided him into her mouth with her left. She paid special attention to its head and slit.

Keylan's head fell back. "Oh, damn…" The way Mia's mouth sucked and pulled had him gripping the sheets. The warmth and wet sensation she offered clouded his mind and curled his toes. Before he could bring himself under control, Mia whispered, "Let go, baby."

Keylan buried his hands in Mia's hair, the thrust of his hips matching her pace, and before long he did just that.

"Damn…" He saw the look of satisfaction on Mia's face as she crawled up his body and laid her head on his chest. He wrapped his arms around her.

Mia couldn't believe how easy and yet necessary it was for her to please Keylan in such a way. How she found her own pleasure pleasing him. She could feel the sting of tears burn the backs of her eyes and she didn't want him to see her crying again, so she tried to move away.

Keylan tightened his grip on her. "Where do you think you're going?" he asked before rolling over on top of her.

"Ummm…"

"That's what I thought. You don't get to run away from me…ever."

"I wasn't running away," she murmured, dropping her eyes like she'd just been caught in a lie.

"Are you upset about anything that we've done?" He wiped away her tears.

Mia captured his gaze. She wanted to make sure he saw how much she meant what she was about to say. "Not at all. I'm happier than I've been in years. So happy, it's scaring me a bit."

Keylan tilted his head slightly. "A bit?"

The corners of her mouth turned up. "Just a bit."

He kissed her passionately on the lips. "I'm a little scared, too, but probably not for the reasons you think."

"What do you mean?"

Keylan rolled off the bed, taking Mia with him. He carried her into the bathroom. "Shower and food first, then we talk." Mia nodded.

"That's some shower you got there."

"You haven't seen the best part," he stated.

"Really, what's that?"

He gifted her with a sexy smile. "Me."

Mia and Keylan shared a sensual shower that left them both spent and hungry.

He dressed Mia in the top of his black silk pajamas while he wore the matching pants. Barefoot, they made their way down to a small galley kitchen that sat off a hall leading to the east wing of the house.

"This place is mostly windows built on the side of mountains near rivers and lakes. You'd think it would be freezing in these halls in spite of the central heat and fireplaces everywhere."

"It's the triple-insulated windows. My aunt hates the cold."

"But your house is built on a mountain."

"It was my mother's idea. She's big on security and privacy, remember?" Keylan said.

"I remember. Why do you have a small kitchen up here?"

"My mother didn't want us kids running up and down the stairs looking for midnight snacks."

"Make sense…I guess."

Keylan directed Mia to a stool. "Have a seat while I get our dinner."

"Dinner?"

"Yes. I had Alice bring it up here. I knew we'd be hungry after working up an appetite," he proclaimed proudly.

Mia giggled and leaned against the counter. "What's for dinner?"

"Spaghetti and some of the best meatballs you've ever had."

Mia gave him a wicked smile. "I doubt that."

Keylan walked up to her, nudged her legs apart with his knee and stepped between her thighs. "Don't remind me of what you can do with that beautiful mouth of yours or we'll never eat." He kissed her as if his life depended on it.

Pulling a covered dish from a warmer, he placed it on a carrying tray. He selected two plates and grabbed some bread. "Can you take that bottle of wine and those two glasses?" He directed Mia to a smaller table.

Mia hopped off the stool. "I sure can." She picked up the bottle and read the label. "Château Lafite Rothschild, nice."

"Let's go."

They returned to Keylan's room, where they ate in bed.

"This is so good," Mia proclaimed.

"Told you," he said, taking a drink from his wineglass.

As they ate, Keylan shared everything that had gone wrong with his trip home. He even told Mia about his conversation with Colby and his need for a big-boy bike, a subject he knew was a touchy one.

"He's four. The bike he has is fine. He needs the training wheels," she insisted.

"Not if he doesn't think so." Keylan broke off a piece of bread and handed it to Mia.

"He's too young to know what's best for him."

"Yes, when it comes to most things. But there are some things kids can and should have a say in."

"Not when it comes to their safety," she insisted, reaching for the bottle and topping off both their glasses.

"You can't smother the boy, Mia."

Mia held up her hands. "Can we change the subject, please?"

"Sure, for now."

"Why are you scared?" She placed her empty plate on the tray.

Keylan put his empty plate next to Mia's, took the tray and set it outside his bedroom door as if he was in an upscale hotel. He returned to the bed, took Mia's hand in his and peered into her eyes. "I was serious when I said I want a future with you and Colby. What scares me is what that would mean for you...for us. Being a Kingsley...being *with* a Kingsley isn't easy."

"I get that—"

"I'm not sure you do, baby. The wealth is a blessing and a curse. People will start to see you differently. They'll respond to who they think you are and what you can do for them. The security, the media, it can all become overwhelming when you're not used to it." He squeezed her hand. "I'm scared to death that you won't be able to handle it all."

"But…" Mia broke eye contact and pushed out a quick breath. "If we love each other, we can handle anything that comes our way, right?"

Keylan pulled her into his arms. "I hope so, my love. I really do, because I'm not letting you go."

Don't cry… Don't cry. "Good."

"Now let's get some sleep, because we have a busy day tomorrow."

"Doing what exactly?" Mia laid her head on Keylan's chest.

"I'm going to show you everything our mountain has to offer. I can't wait to get Colby here. I'd love for him to have a white Christmas," he murmured before drifting off to sleep.

The next morning, Mia woke up naked and alone. At some point in the night they'd made love again and Keylan had let the athlete in him take control. Mia smiled as she remembered flashes of all the different positions Keylan had managed to put her body in. "Keylan… Keylan," she called out.

Mia got up and made her way to the bathroom, every muscle in her body protesting each step she took. After using the restroom and brushing her teeth, Mia stepped into the shower, hoping all those jets would do their job and revive her body.

After several minutes Mia's muscles did, in fact, start to relax and she could sense she was no longer alone.

"Good morning."

Mia turned to find a fully dressed Keylan leaning against the doorjamb. "Good morning. Where have you been?"

"I wanted to get in a few runs down the mountain. I figure you wouldn't be ready to do that just yet."

"I guess that explains the outfit, and you were right." She smiled at how sexy he looked in his black snow pants and long-sleeved white shirt.

Keylan smirked. "I called and checked in on Colby and he's fine. Get dressed and meet me downstairs in the family room."

"Which room is that again?" Mia turned off the water and reached for her towel.

"Damn, you're beautiful." Keylan walked into the bathroom, leaned down and kissed her. "The family room is the one where the window faces the mountains."

Mia's eyebrows rose. "I'm going to need more than that to go on, mister."

"The one with the big pool table across from the stairs."

"Got it."

Keylan walked out of the bathroom. Mia was awestruck by the way his snow pants fit his perfect behind and her body began to stir.

You have got to get a grip, girl.

Mia walked into the closet and selected the white outfit that Sandra had insisted made her look like a Kingsley, though she had no idea what that meant. After drying her body and hair, she dressed in a white turtleneck sweater and white snow pants and pulled her hair into a tight bun. She applied as little makeup as possible and slipped her feet into a pair of boots that had cost more than what anyone should be allowed to pay.

Mia put on the matching white mink-lined jacket and glanced at her reflection in the mirror. She finally knew just what Sandra meant. Mia was wearing a six-thousand-dollar outfit and she didn't look like herself. She looked like a Kingsley. She wasn't sure how she felt about that, no matter how much she loved Keylan.

Being invited into this world of luxury and excess was new to Mia. She had seen firsthand how this changed people; her ex put money and fame before her and Colby. Mia knew she was being ridiculous. Keylan—and the entire Kingsley family, for that matter—had been nothing but generous. She saw every day how they shared their time and resources for the betterment of others. Mia took another look in the mirror and this time she smiled.

Chapter 25

Mia made her way to the family room and spied an off-looking Keylan sitting at a small, round table in the corner of the room reading something on his phone. When he spotted her, he placed his phone aside. "You found it," he said with a half smile as he rose from his chair. "I was about ready to send out a search party." He kissed her on the cheek and helped her out of her jacket, placing it on the back of her chair.

"Everything okay? You look like something is wrong."

"Everything is fine." He relaxed his face and pointed to the mobile tray next to the table. "We have coffee, orange juice and cocoa. What's your pleasure?"

"Coffee and orange juice. Thank you."

Keylan poured up her request and handed them to her. "You look gorgeous, by the way."

Mia accepted the cup and glass. "I feel like a snowman in all this white, but Sandra and the salesperson insisted that I get this one."

"Sandra?"

"Yes." Mia sipped her coffee. "She went shopping with me. She said this outfit made me look like a Kingsley."

"Oh, yeah? What do we Kingsleys look like?"

The corners of her mouth rose and she remembered what he'd said last night. "Money."

Keylan nodded as if his earlier point had been made. He reached for his glass.

"What's that you're drinking?"

"A protein energy drink. Between you and our mountain, I need to replenish." He glanced over at his beeping phone.

"Do you need to get that?"

"Actually—"

"Excuse me, sir, are you ready to order?" a tall, thin young man asked as he entered the room.

"Yes." Keylan waved him forward. "Forgive me, what was your name?"

"Patch," he replied.

"Mia, this is Patch. He's new to the staff," Keylan said by way of introduction.

"Good morning, Patch."

"What would you like for breakfast?" Keylan took a drink from his glass while he waited for Mia's response.

"What do you mean?"

"Pancakes, eggs, steak, maybe? Whatever you want, the kitchen can make," he elaborated.

Mia shrugged and Keylan laughed at her clear confusion. "Patch, we'll have some mixed fruit first, brown sugar and cinnamon oatmeal, and we'll round things off with ham-and-cheese omelets fully loaded. Is that okay, Mia?"

She nodded and watched as Patch wrote everything down before leaving. "What was that?"

"What was what?"

Mia rolled her eyes. "You just placed an order like we were in a restaurant."

"Oh, that."

"Yes, that. What's the deal?"

"That's how breakfast is done. Lunch and dinner are different. Those meals are preset by preference. Alice has the menus prepared based on my requests, but if you'd like something special I'm sure we can make it happen."

"No, I'm following your lead this weekend."

"I like the sound of that." Keylan wiggled his eyebrows.

Patch returned with two bowls of fruit, along with toast and several jams and jellies to choose from.

Keylan's phone rang and he glanced at the screen. "Excuse me, baby, I have to take this." He stepped into the foyer before answering the call. "Mavis, is everything all right?"

"Yes. The doctor just gave him another breathing treatment and we'll be heading back home soon. He's perfectly fine. You didn't tell Mia, did you?"

"No, not yet, but I think I should."

"Not unless you want your trip cut short. That child hasn't had a vacation or any real time to herself since Colby was born. She deserves a couple of days of being a pampered twenty-six-year-old. She *is* being pampered, right?"

"Yes, ma'am, she is."

"Good. Now you go enjoy yourself. I got this. I'll let you know if anything changes."

"Please do, and tell Little Man we love him."

"I will," Mavis promised before hanging up.

Keylan knew Mia would be furious at him for keeping this from her from the time her aunt had first called him. No matter how minor the situation was, Keylan felt like a heel for keeping the information to himself, but he also knew how right her aunt was. Mia deserved a break and to be treated like a queen, and he had every intention of doing just that. He shook off the guilt and returned to the table.

"Everything okay?"

"Just an unexpected development." Before Keylan could return to his chair, Alice entered the room.

"Good morning, Alice."

"Good morning," she replied, placing a large bowl of oatmeal in front of each of them. "Sit down and eat, KJ, before your food gets cold."

Keylan followed her direction. "I can't count the number of times you've told me that over the years, Ms. Alice."

"I can. Way too many to discuss. Did you sleep well, Mia, dear?"

Mia's eyes cut to Keylan, who winked at her. "Yes, ma'am, I did."

"Alice's oatmeal is the best," Keylan related.

"You're making breakfast, too?" Mia asked, taking a bite of her oatmeal.

"Child, no. We have a full staff for that. I just make the oatmeal for everyone."

"This is delicious."

"Thank you."

"Who's everyone?" Mia took another bite.

"I'll leave the explaining to KJ. Eat up and enjoy your day."

Keylan could see the curiosity in Mia's eyes. *I'm not sure how much more Kingsley she can handle, but here goes nothing.* "While this is our family home, during the holidays and summer, the west wing is open for business."

"Business?"

"Yes, it's open to the public. It becomes an upscale, thirty-room resort and spa that celebrities, business associates and politicians frequent. That includes a couple of presidents. Not to mention a few of our own parties and activities are held there, too."

"Just the west wing?"

He nodded slowly. "The main house and the east wing remain private year-round. The west wing has its own parking area and two helicopter pads."

Mia ate in silence and he respected her need for it. He realized that she might finally be grasping the enormity of their wealth and influence and what all that meant. It was a lot to process.

Keylan sat back and finished off his oatmeal.

Mia set down her spoon and pushed her bowl forward. "So it's open now?"

"Yes."

Patch walked in and placed their omelets before them. "Thank you. It looks great." Mia complimented him before he scurried out of the room, leaving them alone. "With such a distinguished guest list, I assume there's press here." Mia used a fork to cut into her omelet and took a bite. "Mmm, so good."

"Celebrities and politicians bring out the press, so yes, but their focus will be on them and not us. Besides, we're staying on our side of the house and the mountain."

"If you say so." Mia wiped her mouth, having finished half of her food. "I'm full. What's on the agenda today?"

"We'll take a quick tour of the west wing, and then it's my lady's choice, skiing or snowboarding down Kingsley Mountain, before we head down to the village for lunch and a little shopping."

"How about we take that quick tour, skip right to the shopping before it's time for lunch?"

Keylan laughed. "Skiing it is."

Mia groaned. "Fine, but if I break something I'm really going to be pissed."

"If you break something, I'll happily play doctor with you," he promised.

Mia rolled her eyes skyward. "Let's get this over with."

Keylan rose, helped Mia out of her chair and pulled her into his arms. "I need this first." He leaned down and Mia went up on her toes, circling her arms around his neck.

Keylan kissed her as if he was afraid he wouldn't get another chance.

"If we keep this up, we'll never get out of here," Mia said, trying to catch her breath.

"Well, let's get started." He led her out a side door, down a long hall and through another set of secured doors that opened into a living area in the west wing of the house.

Keylan showed Mia everything they had to offer in a vacation spot to their foundation kids—the indoor bowling alley, a large movie theater, a game room any kid would be satisfied with and a massive gymnasium. He even showed her their on-site night club that could be easily converted to a kids' dance club.

Mia admitted to not only being surprised but really impressed. "This place really is amazing, and you're right—this would be a great experience for our kids."

"I'm glad you agree. Now…" Keylan looked like the cat that ate several canaries.

Mia gave him the side-eye. "Now…what?"

"Time to hit the slopes."

Mia spent the next two hours on what was considered a junior slope and couldn't believe how much fun she was having, the type of fun she hadn't had in years. She didn't even care that there were reporters who managed to take their picture before being removed by Keylan's security.

"I must admit, that really was great. What's next?"

Keylan laughed. "We're going to a small village at the base of the mountain. There's a few places I'd like to show you." He took Mia's hand and led her out to a waiting SUV where they took the forty-minute drive down the mountain.

The small lakeside village, nestled between two peaks, had fewer than eight hundred inhabitants. It had taken great lengths, with the financial support of the Kingsleys, to ensure its stunning and cozy appeal remained untarnished.

Keylan took great pride in introducing Mia to the villagers. He even showed off pictures of himself with Colby, promising to bring him back for a visit. Mia's heart exploded with love for the man she pictured having a future with.

They made their way to a small, two-bedroom cottage on the outskirts of town. They exited the vehicle and Mia couldn't believe her eyes. "Wow, this place is beautiful." She loved the snow on both the roof and grass and the flickering light in the window. "What is this place? It looks like something you'd see on the front of a beautiful holiday card."

Keylan kissed her hand. "It's home away from home."

They walked up the three wooden steps and Keylan opened the door. Mia was overwhelmed by the warmth and romantic feel of the room. The decorations were what she'd expect in a small country house. It even had a beautiful Christmas tree in the window. A table set for two sat in front of a crackling fireplace.

Keylan closed and locked the door. Mia walked farther into the house and turned to face Keylan. "What's going on?"

"This is the first vacation home my parents bought. My brother and his wife, China, spent their honeymoon here."

Mia bit her lip. "Really?"

"Really," he murmured before pulling Mia into his arms, kissing her with such passion her knees went weak. He scooped Mia up and carried her into a vintage design bedroom. He placed Mia gently on a solid, metal framed, king-size bed and hovered over her. "I want to make love to you. Right here…right now."

"Yes," she whispered, her body already on fire for him.

Clothes were removed and thrown haphazardly across the room.

Keylan came down on top of Mia, kissing his way along her neck to her breasts. He teased her nipples, while his right hand slid between her legs. He inserted one finger, then another, inside her and Mia's hips matched each magical stroke of his hand, pushing her over the edge. He kissed, licked and nibbled his way down her stomach. He used both hands to widen her legs, opening her up to him. Mia watched as he inhaled her scent with his eyes closed.

Keylan raised his head and gazed into her eyes. "You're mine." His voice was low. He lowered his head and devoured her with such passion that before long she began to tremble and her hips rose from the bed. He sent Mia over the edge.

"In…now…inside. Pl-please," she demanded incoherently.

Keylan pulled out a condom from the nightstand and rolled it on before he hovered over Mia, allowing his shaft to tease her sex. "Do you trust me?" he asked, his voice husky and eyes dark with desire.

Keylan looked as though he was ready to ravage her and Mia couldn't wait. "Yes…"

"Do you love me?"

"Yes…please." She wrapped her legs around his waist.

Keylan whispered, "Roll over, baby."

Mia eagerly complied. He pulled her up on her knees and had Mia rest on her forearms. She gripped the bed rails, presenting her backside to him. Keylan kissed and licked his way up her back while he cupped and massaged her breasts. He brushed her hair to the side, snuggled her neck and whispered how much he loved her. He shared in graphic detail all the wicked things he was about to do and Mia was more turned on than ever before.

Keylan gripped Mia's hips with both hands and entered her from behind. His initial slow and deliberate thrust instantly pushed Mia over the edge. He set a pace that had them both savoring the peaks and valleys of pleasure. Together they reached a level of satisfaction that had them both breathing hard and lying flat on their stomachs.

"Are you okay?" Keylan asked, reaching over and brushing her hair from her face. "That was a little intense."

"That was perfect, baby." Mia's stomach growled.

"Hungry?"

Mia smiled. "Very." Keylan's phone rang and his mouth twisted. "You okay?"

"Yes. Check the bathroom. There should be a couple of robes behind the door."

Mia walked into the bathroom and glanced in the mirror. "Girl, you look a mess—happy, but a mess." She bit her bottom lip. "Yep, he's a keeper."

Chapter 26

After reading through Aunt Mavis's latest email, Keylan breathed a sigh of relief. He knew he had to tell Mia what was going on with Colby, and soon. Keylan didn't want there to be secrets between them, especially when it pertained to her son, but he also knew the moment he told Mia what was going on with Colby, no matter how much he tried to convince her that he was fine, she'd insist on cutting their trip short. *Give her one more day. She deserves it.* He placed his phone on the nightstand and went to join Mia in the bathroom. After cleaning themselves up and wrapping their bodies in a pair of thick robes, they made their way over to the small kitchen.

"So what's for...?" She checked the time on the microwave. "Oh, man, it's almost six, so I guess it's dinnertime."

"Yeah, we slept through lunch." Keylan opened the oven door and removed a warm pan of chicken and rice.

"That looks good." Mia moved over to a cabinet and pulled down two plates. "How much time do we have before the car comes back for us?"

"All night," he replied, taking a bottle of wine from the refrigerator before removing two glasses from another cabinet.

"What?"

"They'll pick us up in the morning. Being here with you feels special."

"Why didn't we just come here in the first place?"

"You needed to see The Resort, remember?" he reminded.

They sat in front of the fireplace and ate. Mia marveled at the snow that had just begun to fall. "Beautiful," she said.

"Yes, you are," Keylan said.

"I was referring to the snow." Mia placed another bite of food in her mouth.

"I wasn't."

"Let me see your phone. I want to call and check in on Colby. He would just love to play in this snow."

"I'm sure he would. It's in the bedroom. I'll go get it." He retrieved his phone and handed it to Mia.

Mia took another bite of her food before accepting the phone and placing her call.

Keylan sat back expressionless as he watched Mia dial her aunt. He knew she would be mad once she found out that he'd withheld information about Colby but he was sure she'd understand. He hoped that she would, anyway. This was the first break Mia had had in years, and he wanted her to relax and enjoy herself. She had to know she wasn't alone anymore. Everything was going to be fine. After all, they loved each other. *I'll come clean tomorrow.*

"Keylan? Keylan…" Mia called, holding his phone out to him.

"Sorry." He took the phone back and placed it facedown on the table.

"Where did you go?"

"Nowhere, just tired, I guess." He finished off his wine.

"Aunt Mavis said Colby was asleep. Apparently, he and Uncle Rudy had a busy day."

"Really?"

"Yes, it seems more gifts arrived today." Mia tilted her head and quirked her left eyebrow. "You're going to spoil him."

"A little bit," he promised.

Mia stood, walked around the table and sat in Keylan's lap. She wrapped her arms around his neck and said, "Why don't we go back to bed so I can spoil you a little bit?"

They spent the rest of the night enjoying each other in multiple ways before falling asleep wrapped in each other's arms.

The next morning, Mia was still so exhausted from their night of aggressive lovemaking that she was certain she'd sleep the entire trip back to The Resort.

Keylan left Mia alone to change while he went to get everything ready for their return trip home. He returned to the bedroom and found a blue-jeans-and-sweater-clad Mia sitting on the bed. Her arms and legs were crossed, her nose in the air and her jaw set.

She knows.

"Do you want to tell me what the hell you were thinking?" Mia was finding it hard to keep her emotions in check when all she wanted to do was scream.

Keylan started approaching her. "Your aunt assured me—"

"Don't!" Mia held up her right hand and he stopped in his tracks.

"Colby was fine. We didn't want to spoil our getaway."

"So you, the man that claims to love me, lied to me."

"Claims." His jaw clenched. "I do love you, and I didn't lie to you."

"You just withheld vital information from me about *my* son." She pointed at herself. Mia couldn't deal with any kind of secrets or half truths when it came to her son, no matter how good the intentions.

"I agreed with your aunt that waiting to tell you would be the best option so you wouldn't overreact. Like now."

"You think my being angry about this is an overreaction." She placed her right hand on her hip.

"Yes, as a matter of fact, I do. Your aunt had everything under control and she didn't need you hovering."

"I'm his mother, dammit. It's my job to protect him. You're not a parent, so you can't understand."

"Of course it is, and I don't have to be a parent to understand, but you're not doing that job alone. Everything doesn't have to be taken to the extreme."

"So you think my feelings are extreme."

"Yes...I do."

"Then you're really going to love this." Mia reached behind her back, picked up her phone and tossed it to him. "Check out those headlines. How do *you* think I should react to that?"

Keylan looked down at the phone, which was open to an internet browser. "Oh, God..."

Mia folded her arms. "My personal favorite is the shot of the two of us on the slopes with the headline 'Mia Ramirez Enjoys a Lavish Holiday While Son in Hospital.' Oh, yeah, and of course the one that says, 'Mia Ramirez Chooses Sex Over Her Sick Son.'"

"Mia, you can't pay attention to this garbage. We talked about this." He came and sat next to her on the bed.

"Yes, and you keep saying the same thing. It doesn't matter, I should ignore it."

"Because you should, and sooner or later they go away and focus on someone else."

Mia rose and walked into the closet. "You just don't get it." She started packing her clothes. "My son was sick and you didn't tell me, and that lack of knowledge is splattered all over the internet. What if something had happened to him?"

Keylan followed her into the closet. "Nothing did, but you have to know that if it had, I would have told you and moved heaven and earth to get you to him," he said, placing his hands in his pockets.

"No, I don't know that, and something bad could have happened. Bad things happen all the time, and you had no right to make decisions regarding *my* kid for me. You're not his father and all the money in the world doesn't make it so." Those words left a bitter aftertaste but Mia was too angry to do anything about it.

"You're right, I'm not, but I love him, too."

"So do his doctors. Can you call for the car? I want to go home. Now!"

Keylan nodded, turned and walked out the room.

The helicopter ride to the airport and the plane trip home were made in mostly silence. Mia couldn't figure out what she was angrier about: the fact that Keylan had decided she didn't need to know her son was sick, the idea that she was being labeled an unfit mother or the hurtful words she'd said to Keylan when he'd been more of a father to Colby than his biological father. Mia wanted to kick herself for the hurtful words she'd used and the possible hurt they might have caused but she was just too overwhelmed by all the emotions she was feeling: anger, betrayal and love.

She walked into her house to find the Christmas presents under the tree had tripled. Her aunt greeted her with a big hug. "Hello, sweetheart. I hope you haven't given this man too hard of a time."

"It's fine, Aunt Mavis," Keylan assured her, setting Mia's luggage down and keeping his distance.

"Aunt Mavis, how's Colby?"

Before she could respond she heard, "Mommy... Keylan."

Mia knelt and Colby ran into her outstretched arms. The moment she felt his heartbeat against hers, a calming wave came over her. The pain in her chest had eased but it hadn't disappeared. "Mommy missed you, man. How do you feel?"

"I'm good. Keylan."

Colby wiggled away from his mother and ran into Keylan's arms. "Hey, buddy. I'm happy you're feeling better."

"I did what you said."

"I know." Keylan stood and ran his hand through Colby's hair.

Mia frowned.

"Keylan told Colby to be like steel...like a superhero, while the doctors gave him his breathing treatments," her aunt explained.

Mia turned to face Keylan. "You told him that?"

"Yes." His jaw set. "We were trying to shield you from unnecessary worry, not him from us. I figured one parent figure was good enough for a day or so. I guess I was wrong."

"Oh..." Mia returned her attention to Colby, feeling even more confused.

"Keylan, let's play."

"I'm sorry, man, I have to go. I have a plane to catch."

"You're leaving?" Mia's heart dropped.

"Yes, I have to get to California. We have a game tomorrow night." He smiled at Colby. "I'll call you, man, and come see you when I get back—" he looked over at Mia "—if it's okay with your mom."

"Okeydoke."

"Back to bed," Aunt Mavis said, following after him.

"I should go." Keylan turned for the door.

Mia nodded. "Thanks for everything. I'm sorry things had to end—"

"It's fine." Keylan leaned down, kissed her on the cheek and walked out the door.

Mia brought her left hand to her cheek and held it there as she watched Keylan drive away.

"Did Keylan leave?" Aunt Mavis asked, walking into the living room.

Mia nodded, unable to get words past the lump in her throat. Her feelings of anger and sadness were in a battle of wills and Mia had no idea which team she was rooting for. Mia collected her bags and brought them farther into the living room.

Mavis stood in her path with her hands on her hips. "Where do you think you're going, young lady?"

"I'm going to go put my things away."

"No, you're not. Sit down."

"Auntie—"

Mavis narrowed her eyes at Mia and said, "Sit...down!"

Mia reluctantly complied. She felt like a child about to be scolded for something she'd done wrong and in that moment she wasn't sure if she actually hadn't.

"That man, the one that you basically just 'kicked to the curb,' as you young people say, is about the best thing that has ever happened to both you and Colby."

"Auntie, he—"

"He what? Didn't tell you that Colby was sick? That's because I asked him not to," she explained.

"And why would you do that?" Mia's tone harder than she intended.

"Because you needed this break. You haven't had one moment to yourself, let alone in the company of a man who loves you, since you brought that beautiful boy home," she said, pointing to the area where Mia's son slept.

"I'm his mother. Keylan's not even his biological father." Mia's eyes filled with tears and she brought her hands to her heart. It was beating so hard she felt as if she had to keep it from bursting through her chest. "I'm the one that's been there whenever he's been sick. The one that's supposed to be there—that's my job."

Mavis tilted her head slightly. "By your logic, because your uncle Rudy and I aren't your biological parents, we shouldn't have been the ones that nursed and cared for you all those times you got sick. We shouldn't have been your only support system, holding your hand through all Colby's doctor's appointments and hospitalizations. I mean, we're not his grandparents—you're my niece and he's my great-nephew. The fact that we raised you…loved you…doesn't count. Right?" Her comments were laced in sarcasm. Mavis was clearly trying to send Mia a message.

Mia lowered her head and dropped her hands. Her tears were flowing too fast to even try and swipe them away. She knew what her aunt was trying to say. "I… I just…"

"Just what? I know you trust us with Colby." She reached for Mia's hand and squeezed it.

"Of course I do," Mia replied, looking up at her aunt. "And I know nurture supersedes nature. You and Uncle Rudy are the best parents I could have or ever want."

Mavis freed her hand, reached for the Kleenex box that sat on the table behind the sofa and handed it to Mia. "Then what's this really about? You have to know if something was seriously wrong with Colby, I would have told you and Keylan would have had you by his side in no time."

Mia dropped her shoulders and sighed before saying in a voice barely above a whisper, "I just don't want to be like her."

"Who?" Mavis frowned.

"My mother," she confessed.

"Oh, sweetheart." Mavis pulled her into her arms and Mia laid her head against her aunt's shoulder and cried. "You're nothing like your mother."

"I don't know." Mia shook her head.

"I do. My sister was young and she had…issues. She knew her limitations and did the best thing possible for you. Your mother gave you to people who would love and cherish you. You are the highlight of our life. I never thought I'd have a child. You made that dream come true and you didn't come from me."

Mia burst out laughing and raised her head. "Auntie…"

Mavis's cell phone beeped. "Wipe your nose," she ordered as she reached for her phone. After responding to the text she said, "Your uncle is so spoiled. Anyway, where were we?"

"I just don't want Colby to ever think I did or would leave him for anything or anyone."

"Sweet child, your son loves you so much and he knows how much you love him. But being overprotective isn't good for either of you. Colby enjoys having a little independence. And I hate to break it to you, but your uncle and I had everything under control and Colby was fine. The only reason Colby spoke to Keylan is because Keylan insisted on it."

"He did?" Mia bit her lip.

"Yes, he wanted to make sure Colby was okay and that he knew you'd be home soon. If Colby had asked for you, he would have told you everything and brought you back. He loves Colby."

"He really does love Colby." The dam she'd erected to hold back additional tears broke. "Oh, Auntie, I think I blew it."

"Sweetie." She pulled Mia into her arms. "That man loves you."

Mia nodded. "We had a fight and I said some horrible things."

"Just give him some time. I'm sure this won't be your last disagreement."

"I don't know."

"I do. I'm sure it'll blow over in a few days." She wiped away her tears. "It's almost Christmas, and magical things happen this time of year. Now, I'm going to head home and you should get some rest. You do have work tomorrow."

"Thanks for everything, Auntie."

Keylan spent most of the night thinking about his fight with Mia. He tried to rest on the plane but his mind kept reliving their argument. He wanted to call her and try to clear the air between them, but he was afraid he'd just make things worse.

He didn't understand why she couldn't see what he'd done was for her own good. He knew firsthand how an overbearing and overprotective mother could mess with a boy's head, and Colby was no different.

He really couldn't believe that she actually thought that if something was seriously wrong with Colby, he wouldn't have moved a mountain to get her to him. That and the fact that she kept letting the media get to her made him wonder if he'd prepared her enough for what happened when someone was in love with a Kingsley.

Keylan usually found solace in arriving early at the visiting team's arena especially after tossing and turning most of the night. He enjoyed being in their house, admiring any victory banners they may have, spending time alone on their court, dropping down threes or just sitting along the sidelines, soaking in the atmosphere that fueled him for the job before him. But now all he wanted to do was to talk to Mia. He was making his way to the locker room when he ran into Roger.

"There you are."

"What's up?" Keylan kept bouncing the basketball he had been using.

"I was concerned after your call last night. It seems a lot happened over the weekend. I was just checking to see if you are okay."

"I'm good." Keylan captured the ball in his hands and screamed, "I'm good!" before throwing the ball across the court.

"Wow. Sure you are. Sit for a minute."

Keylan plopped down in a nearby seat and lowered his face into his hands. "Man, you have got to pull it together before tonight. You can't take this out on the court."

Keylan dropped his shoulders and his hands. He leaned back in the chair and said, "You're right."

"Look, those headlines about Mia were harsh, but it's something she'll have to get used to."

"I tried to explain that to her, but she doesn't seem to get it."

Roger sighed. "She doesn't get it, or you don't?"

Keylan sat up in the chair. "What are you talking about? I've dealt with media vultures my whole life."

"Yes, you have, but she hasn't. No amount of preparation can really prepare you for that level of invasion of privacy. And your nonchalant and dismissive attitude toward it doesn't help."

"I thought you were on my side."

"I am, and you've made it very clear that Mia is your future, so it's up to you to make sure she gets through the bumps she'll face getting to that future. One more thing— not telling Mia about her sick son was a bonehead move. Take the L on that one."

"You know how much I hate to lose." The corners of his mouth rose.

"I know."

Keylan smirked. "Thanks, Roger." He stood and they bumped fists.

"Just doing my job."

"You're a great agent, but you're an even better friend."

"I know," Roger agreed.

"Time for me to go to work."

Chapter 27

Mia was trying to stay strong and fighting back tears as she sat next to her son's hospital bed. It was Monday evening and she still couldn't believe they were there so soon after Colby had been to the doctor on Saturday. Watching him sleep through the breathing treatment gave her some solace. She didn't want him to see how scared and upset she really was; she knew how intuitive her son was when it came to her emotions. She didn't want to scare him, especially since he was handling this bout so bravely. Mia had no doubt that that was due to Keylan's influence.

The door to Colby's room opened and the last person she expected entered, dressed in Prada head to toe. Her blue suit only accentuated her powerful aura. "Mia, my dear, how is he?"

Mia stood. "Mrs. Kingsley." She knew her shock at her presence had to be written all over her face. Victoria wasn't exactly the warm and fuzzy type.

"I told you, it's Victoria," she reminded.

"Yes, ma'am. He's doing much better, thank you."

"I understand from my sister he got sick at school today."

"Yes. The fluctuation of our Houston weather can be hard on his little system."

Her expression dulled. "But he's going to be fine, right?"

Mia recognized something in Victoria in that moment. It was in her very expressive eyes and it was something Mia knew she rarely exposed…fear. Maybe it was the mother in Mia that allowed her to recognize it, or maybe it was simply Victoria's guard slipping long enough to show her she wasn't alone. Either way, it helped.

"He should be. The doctors just wanted to run a few more tests to make sure there're no underlying issues with his heart."

The respiratory therapist walked into the room. "Excuse me, ladies," she said, stepping around them and approaching the bed. She turned off the machine and removed the oxygen mask. She made several notes in her tablet before listening to Colby's chest. "Everything sounds good, Mom."

Mia heaved an audible sigh. "Thank you."

"You're very welcome. I'll be back in four hours."

Mia nodded but Victoria's forehead creased. "Four hours?"

"Yes, he has to have breathing treatments every four hours for a full twenty-four hours. That's only his second one."

"Poor thing. That must be really hard on him."

"Usually, but Keylan…taught him how to handle it." The words caught in her throat. She stood over her son's bed and lightly ran her hand through his hair.

"Where's your aunt? You're handling this alone?"

"Yes, but it's fine." Mia forced a smile. "She and my uncle left for their vacation this morning."

"Please sit down. Mind if I join you for a while?"

"Not at all." Mia sat with her hands intertwined in her lap.

Victoria pulled up a chair and sat next to her. "Does my son know that Colby's here? He would want to know… He'd want to be here."

Mia shook her head. She was struggling to get the words past the lump in her throat. She had lost count of the number of times she'd called Keylan in her mind. The number of ways she'd apologized, wishing that he wasn't working and could be with her, holding her hand, but most of all she wished she hadn't thrown all his kindness back in his face.

Mia lowered her head as she had lost her battle to keep her tears in their ducts. "He'd want to hear about Colby but not talk to me. We had a fight and I said some horrible things that I didn't mean," Mia explained, keeping her head down.

Victoria laughed, reached into her purse and pulled out a monogrammed handkerchief. She handed it to Mia and crossed her legs. "My dear, look at me."

Mia slowly lifted her head.

"Keylan James Kingsley is *my* son. If he can't take a few harsh words from the woman he loves, he doesn't deserve you."

"Thank you, but it's not just the fight. The media—"

"Is a necessary evil in our world. And as long as you're a part of it, you'll have to understand that and learn how to deal with it."

"That's just it—I'm not sure I can."

Victoria reached for Mia's hand and squeezed it. "Do you love my son?"

A wide smile spread across Mia's face. "Very much."

"Good, then together you can handle anything."

Victoria's cell phone rang and she pulled it out of her purse. After reading the name, she said, "Excuse me for a moment." She rose and stepped slightly away from Mia. "Thank you for getting back to me so quickly. While I appreciate everything you've done, in the future I'd expect for you both to stick to our agreement and not deviate."

Mia wasn't trying to eavesdrop but she couldn't help

but hear Victoria's side of the conversation and know she wasn't happy with whomever she was speaking to. Mia knew Victoria was a powerful woman but seeing her in action was something to behold.

"I appreciate that, and please share my hope for your boss's continued success in her new role as commissioner." Victoria ended the call and returned her phone to her purse. "Now, where was I? Oh, yes, I'm having Colby moved to a VIP room, which has a bed for you. You need to get some rest, and we both know you're not leaving his side."

"That's not necessary."

Victoria walked over to Colby's bed. She leaned down and kissed him on the forehead before turning back to face Mia. "It most certainly is. Nothing's too good for my future grandson."

Future grandson. Mia knew better than to argue with Victoria, but she figured that any future she'd hoped to have with Keylan was pretty much off the table. "Thank you."

"Kirby and her team are in place. If you need anything, just let her or me know."

"I will, thank you."

Within an hour Colby had been moved to a large room that rivaled any kid's fantasy. Between the rocket-ship-shaped bed, the large chalkboard wall and box of toys waiting for attention, any kid would be motivated to get better.

The beautiful daybed was a welcome sight for Mia.

After ensuring that Colby was resting comfortably, she changed out of her work clothes and into a pair of black leggings and a black Carriers T-shirt thanks to Kirby, who'd collected a few things from her house. Exhausted physically and mentally, Mia laid across the bed and was asleep in seconds.

"Man, you were on fire tonight. What a way to come back, with a triple double… Twenty-five points, fifteen rebounds and ten assists tonight. You clearly got your focus back." Roger praised Keylan.

"You know me, man. I can compartmentalize." Keylan slipped on his suit jacket and began packing his bag. "Besides, we're headed home and I'm going to talk to Mia."

"Yeah, about Mia…" Roger fretted.

"What about her?" Keylan's face went blank.

Roger explained Colby's current hospitalization. Keylan's knees buckled and he gripped his locker to keep himself upright. His chest was tight and he was finding it difficult to fill his lungs.

Keylan pulled out his phone and tried to call Mia, only to be sent to her voice mail. "Dammit!"

"Nothing?"

"No, it keeps going to voice mail." Keylan's phone rang and he looked down, hoping it was Mia returning his call.

"Not now."

"What is it?" Roger frowned.

"My mother," he uttered.

"You should get that," he directed.

"Why?"

"Because she was the one who told me about Mia."

"Yes, Mother?" Keylan answered, his desperation on full display.

"Have you spoken to Roger?"

"Yes, ma'am."

"So you're on the way to the airport?"

"No, our plane doesn't leave for several more hours," he explained.

"That's why I sent the jet. It's waiting for you at the airport."

"Is Colby okay?"

"Yes," she said.

"And Mia?"

"About as well as can be expected. Just get to the airport."

"Thanks, Mother." Keylan disconnected the call and turned to Roger. "Meet me outside. I have to go talk to Coach."

"I'll have the car brought around."

Mia opened her eyes to a dimly lit room. As soon as her eyes made the proper adjustments, she reached for her phone to check the time, only to see that she'd missed several calls from Keylan. "You left your phone on mute and missed the chance to talk to Keylan. Just great...nice going, Mia."

"No, you didn't, baby."

Mia sprang forward. She scanned the room to find a dark figure rising from a chair in the corner next to Colby's bed. He walked into what little light the room had and came to sit next to Mia on the bed. "Wh-what are you doing here?"

"My family needed me," he proclaimed.

Mia threw her arms around his neck and kissed him. "I'm sorry about what I said."

"I'm sorry. You were right—I should have told you what was happening with Colby."

"You were right, too. I can be overprotective and stubborn, and I shouldn't let the media get to me so much. I'll work on it. I promise."

Keylan kissed her again. "How's our boy?"

Mia's heart started racing at his words. *Our boy.* "He's fine. The tests look good. I can take him home tomorrow."

"We can take him home tomorrow. Speaking of which..." Keylan took Mia's hand in his. "I know it's fast, but I love you and Colby. We belong together, Mia, and I want us to be a family."

"Are you sure?" Her voice was low.

"Yes, and my question to you is, can you handle becoming a member of my family and all that comes with it?"

"I love you so much and I know Colby loves you, too. Yes, I can handle it, with your help."

Keylan hugged and kissed Mia until they both had a need for air. "As soon as he's well enough, I want to find a justice of the peace to make our family legal. I want to start the process of making Colby legally my son. I want him to have my name."

"You want to adopt Colby?"

"Yes, of course. If you want a wedding—"

"I just want us to be a family."

"Good, because I want that, too…but by Christmas," he declared.

Mia laughed, wiping at a fresh set of tears. "You do realize that's next week."

Keylan pulled Mia onto his lap and kissed her lightly on the lips. "Yes, I do, my love. What a wonderful and unexpected gift."

* * * * *

If you enjoyed this romantic story,
don't miss these other titles by Martha Kennerson:

PROTECTING THE HEIRESS
SEDUCING THE HEIRESS
TEMPTING THE HEIRESS
ALWAYS MY BABY

Available now from Harlequin Kimani Romance!

COMING NEXT MONTH
Available December 19, 2017

#553 PLAYING WITH SEDUCTION
Pleasure Cove • by Reese Ryan

Premier event promoter Wesley Adams is glad to be back in North Carolina. Until he discovers the collaborator on his next venture is competitive volleyball player Brianna "Bree" Evans, the beauty he spent an unforgettable evening with more than a year ago. Will their past cost them their second chance?

#554 IT'S ALWAYS BEEN YOU
The Jacksons of Ann Arbor • by Elle Wright

Best friends Dr. Lovely "Love" Washington and Dr. Drake Jackson wake up in a Vegas hotel to discover not only did they become overnight lovers, they're married. But neither remembers tying the knot. Will they finally realize what's been in front of them all along—true love?

#555 OVERTIME FOR LOVE
Scoring for Love • by Synithia Williams

Between school, two jobs and caring for her nephew, Angela Bouler is keeping it all together…until Isaiah Reynolds bounces into her life. Angela's hectic life doesn't quite mesh with the basketball star's image of the perfect partner. Winning her heart won't be easy, but it's the only play that matters…

#556 SOARING ON LOVE
The Cardinal House • by Joy Avery

Tressa Washington will do anything to escape the disastrous aftermath of her engagement party. Even stow away in the back of Roth Lexington's car and drive off with the aerospace engineer. In his snowbound cabin, they'll learn that to reach the heights of love, they'll have to be willing to fall…